Aucassin
and
Nicolette

fuoz ce poile moa faus a

ic° k̊ & je deluif amxe bo

Oz fr anev e ...

Tuoalinf fen eft coz nef

tón folmui° ə abof tuef

claméé aleuuf obn

uf nete puivt conformr

e mel bon conbel dou

er-f le prlaifeft atuf

len maten lof & gr̄ep

n f ne ambivx eft- euif

iav moia a ploxev

fu mie aue grvev

Aucassin and Nicolette

and

Nicolette

A FACING-PAGE EDITION AND TRANSLATION

by Robert S. Sturges

MICHIGAN STATE UNIVERSITY PRESS · *East Lansing*

♻ The paper used in this publication meets the minimum requirements
of ansi/niso z39.48-1992 (R 1997) (Permanence of Paper).

Michigan State University Press
East Lansing, Michigan 48823-5245

Printed and bound in the United States of America.

20 19 18 17 16 15 14   1 2 3 4 5 6 7 8 9 10

LIBRARY OF CONGRESS CATALOGING-IN-PUBLICATION DATA
Aucassin et Nicolette. English & French.
Aucassin and Nicolette : a facing-page edition and translation by Robert S.
Sturges.
pages cm
Includes bibliographical references.
Parallel text in English and Old French.
ISBN 978-1-61186-157-0 (pbk.: alk. paper)—ISBN 978-1-60917-443-9 (pdf)—
ISBN 978-1-62895-135-6 (epub)—ISBN 978-1-62896-135-5 (mobi/prc)
I. Sturges, Robert Stuart, 1953–
PQ1426.E5S78 2014
841'.1—dc23
2014028221

Book design by Charlie Sharp, Sharp Des!gns
Cover design by Shaun Allshouse, www.shaunallshouse.com
COVER IMAGE: Heidelberg University Library, Cod. Pal. germ. 848, Grosse
Heidelberger Liederhandschrift (Codex Manesse), folio 249v, Herr Konrad
von Altstetten. Used with permission.

PAGE xx: Bibliothèque nationale de France, fonds français 2168, folio 72r.
This folio includes the text and music for section 7. Facsimile image from C'est
dAucasī & de Nicolete, ed. F. W. Bourdillon (Oxford: Clarendon, 1896), courtesy
of Special Collections, Arizona State University Libraries.

Michigan State University Press is a member of the Green Press Initiative and is
committed to developing and encouraging ecologically responsible publishing
practices. For more information about the Green Press Initiative and the use
of recycled paper in book publishing, please visit www.greenpressinitiative.org.

Visit Michigan State University Press at www.msupress.org

For my favorite translators,

Cynthia Hogue and Sylvain Gallais

Contents

ACKNOWLEDGMENTS

I worked on this edition and translation while teaching at two institutions, the University of New Orleans and Arizona State University. I thank both for the institutional support that helped make this project possible, and I am particularly grateful to the two chairs who approved sabbatical leaves, Maureen Goggin of ASU's English Department and the late John Cooke of UNO's. I also thank my UNO students in two classes on "Mardi Gras, Carnival, and the Carnivalesque," in which I tested the translation at an early stage of development; Lauren Harrison's comments were particularly helpful. I have presented some of the ideas in the introduction at conferences, and I thank the audiences at the MLA convention in Washington, DC, in 2005 and at the University of Aberystwyth in 2000 for their suggestions. Thanks also to the sympathetic and sharp-eyed reader for Michigan State University Press. I am pleased that I can now thank her by name: Molly Lynde-Recchia. And heartfelt thanks to designers Shaun Allshouse and Charles Sharp, as well as to the Michigan State University Press staff for making the publication process painless and even enjoyable, especially Gabriel Dotto, Elise Jajuga, and Kristine M. Blakeslee. Finally, thanks to my husband Jim Davidson for his careful reading.

x

Introduction

Aucassin and Nicolette is one of the comic masterpieces of medieval literature.[1] It survives in a single, late thirteenth-century manuscript (fonds français 2168) in the Bibliothèque national français, in Paris. The manuscript is a collection primarily of romances, lais, and fabliaux, with a few religious texts included as well.[2] The author of Aucassin and Nicolette is anonymous, and identifies himself in the opening lines only as the "viel antif," or old man (section 1). His familiarity with the various literary themes and genres that he parodies (see "Genre and Literary Relations," below), as well as his skillful versifying additionally suggest that he may have been a jongleur, a professional entertainer whose skills might include poetic recitation and composition. Judging by the Old French dialect in which Aucassin and Nicolette is written, its author lived in northern France, specifically Picardy, probably in the first half of the thirteenth century. The tale's mockery of the noble classes has sometimes been taken to indicate that it was intended for a bourgeois or even lower-class audience, though this is by no means certain.[3]

Genre and Literary Relations

The final lines of Aucassin and Nicolette refer to the work as a cantefable, usually translated into modern French as "chantefable" or, in English, "song-story" (section 41). The author thus categorizes it by its unique form, the alternation between verse passages of a varying number of seven-syllable lines, intended to be sung, and prose passages to be recited. It is the only known work to be given this performance-based designation, though other medieval texts, such as Boethius's Consolation of Philosophy and Dante's La Vita nuova, also alternate between verse and prose.[4] That Aucassin and Nicolette was intended to be performed in some way is clear from the text itself: the verse sections after the first are introduced with the phrase "Or se cante" ("Now it is sung"), and in the manuscript most of them are accompanied, in their first two lines, by musical notation indicating alternating melodic lines; that is, the same two lines of music are to be repeated throughout each section of verse, with a brief concluding cadence notated with the shorter final line of each verse section. Within this repeated overall structure, the performer would likely have been free to improvise. Transcriptions of the music in medieval notation can be found in Bourdillon's facsimile edition.[5]

The prose passages are introduced with the phrase "Or dient et content et fablent"

("Now they speak and tell and recount"), also suggesting oral performance. For these reasons, *Aucassin and Nicolette*, although not a play, has sometimes been discussed in terms of drama. It may have been performed by more than one individual, and Grace Frank points out that it illustrates how "the dividing line between the recitation of narrative material and the dramatization of such material was frequently a narrow one" in the Middle Ages.[6]

It is also possible to categorize *Aucassin and Nicolette* in terms of its content and literary relations rather than its form: it imitates and parodies both the epic-heroic genre of *chanson de geste* and the courtly one of romance. Indeed, Sarah Kay has suggested that it parodies the very concept of generic norms themselves.[7] In terms of the *chanson de geste*, the initial setting of the tale is the siege of Beaucaire, and Aucassin's father, Count Garin, encourages him to behave like an epic hero in combating the enemy and protecting his property (section 2); later adventures include capture by seafaring Saracens (section 34), the traditional enemy of Christianity in crusading epics (and indeed in the Crusades themselves). The *chansons de geste* would also have been sung or chanted, like the verse sections of *Aucassin and Nicolette*. But the tone of the latter is far from that of a real *chanson de geste*, especially because Aucassin fails to behave like a proper epic hero: although capable of successful military action on the battlefield, he is perfectly prepared to sacrifice his homeland to the enemy unless his father consents to his forbidden love for Nicolette (sections 8–10). In the hands of the Saracens, Aucassin also behaves less than heroically: he is tossed into the ship's hold and rescued not by his own actions but by a chance shipwreck (section 34). It is, indeed, Nicolette rather than Aucassin who performs the *chantefable*'s heroic actions: whereas Aucassin, more often than not, passively weeps and pines for her, she takes dramatic action, escaping first from her imprisonment in the tower (sections 12–17) and later from her own Saracen captors, making her way back to Aucassin disguised as a *jongleur* (sections 38–40).[8]

These actions of Nicolette's suggest something of the way in which the text parodies romance as well as epic. In one sense, *Aucassin and Nicolette* might be seen as a typical romance, though funnier than most: it follows one of the tried and true romance plots in which lovers are separated by social conventions but manage to overcome them, leading to a wedding at the end. But these two lovers behave as unexpectedly for the romance genre as for the epic. As Caroline A. Jewers has suggested, "its deviation from the form of romance allows for a privileged vantage point from which to view convention and constitutes another form of generic distance from the body of texts it comically reflects."[9] A conventional romance lady, for example, might insist that her lover perform love service to prove that he is worthy of her love, and his service would conventionally consist of adventures—combat with other knights, for instance—demonstrating his prowess. But again, Nicolette is the more adventurous of the two, and requires no love service of Aucassin, who slays no dragons for his lady. On the other hand, Aucassin's devotion to the "courtly love" that often serves to motivate romance heroes can seem excessive; as Norris Lacy points out, Aucassin is "a character in love not only with Nicolette but also, perhaps, with the notion of courtly love."[10] If *Aucassin and Nicolette* parodies the *chanson de geste* by refusing to allow its hero to conform to heroic expectations, it parodies romance at least partly by exaggerating courtly expectations: Aucassin is single-mindedly devoted to his lady, even to the point of paralysis at certain key moments. One might well say that Aucassin's romance-flavored courtliness negates the possibility of his performing as a recognizable hero of either epic or romance.

Aucassin and Nicolette is thus better considered a burlesque than either a proper romance or a *chanson de geste*. In the episode in which the lovers find themselves in the strange land of Torelore (sections 28–34), it also burlesques travel narratives. The later European Middle Ages produced numerous examples of literature (both fictional and nonfictional, though these categories were somewhat more flexible for medieval than for modern readers) describing exotic lands and monstrous peoples. Indeed, one of the most famous nonfiction travel narratives was roughly contemporary with *Aucassin and Nicolette*: the thirteenth-century *Travels* of Marco Polo. Less sober accounts of the geographically and physiologically marginal races beloved of the medieval imagination may have provided the inspiration for Torelore, which parodies them by turning expectations upside down in carnivalesque fashion.[11] This is especially true where gender is concerned: the king of Torelore appears to give birth (section 29), while the queen leads their troops in a battle—which itself turns out to be something more like a food fight than real warfare (sections 30–32). The knights of Torelore thus violate romance expectations not only of gender, but of chivalric class behavior as well. Even Aucassin's personality is turned upside down in Torelore, where for once he performs militarily like a real epic hero—only to find out that such behavior is deemed inappropriate in this carnivalesque kingdom (section 32). Such gender inversions were monstrosities familiar from imaginative accounts of travel, but whereas elsewhere they are treated with wonder and respect, in *Aucassin and Nicolette* they are played for laughs.[12] As a parodic version of travel narrative, Torelore thus imagines an alternative to European class and gender identities. Not surprisingly, Nicolette, who oscillates between conventionally feminine and masculine behavior as well as between different religious and class identities (see "Gender, Race, Religion, and Class" below), finds herself right at home in Torelore—whose inhabitants even want to make her their princess (section 32).

HISTORICAL CONTEXTS

Except for the relatively brief period of time the lovers spend in Torelore, most of the action of *Aucassin and Nicolette* occurs in real places. Beaucaire, where Aucassin's father is the count and Nicolette's owner/guardian a viscount, is a town in southern France that one might still visit today. And the siege of Beaucaire with which the *chantefable* begins has a real historical counterpart as well: the only significant battle in which the real Beaucaire was ever involved during the Middle Ages was the siege of May 1216, undertaken by Simon de Montfort and ten thousand infantrymen (the same number mentioned in *Aucassin and Nicolette*, section 2) in the context of the Albigensian Crusade. Like the battle described in the *chantefable*, the historical siege ended in a truce (section 10).[13]

The Albigensian Crusade was not a crusade against Muslims for the recovery of the Holy Land in the Middle East, but was undertaken by the medieval Church against the so-called Cathar or "Albigensian" heretics who had become influential in southern France. The town of Beaucaire, where *Aucassin and Nicolette* begins and ends, was a heretical stronghold, and was also implicated in the Albigensian Crusade's immediate cause: Pope Innocent III preached the Crusade in response to the assassination of a papal legate, which was believed to have been carried out by a citizen of Beaucaire.[14] There is no mention of the heresy or of the Crusade in the text itself, nor any indication that Aucassin or his family should be considered heretics; but Aucassin does voice some comically unorthodox religious beliefs near the beginning of the *chantefable*, expressing a preference for Hell over Heaven because he imagines the inhabitants of Hell are more interesting (section 6). *Aucassin and Nicolette*'s humor, then, may be a way of dealing with, or defusing, real-world anxieties about the heretics' challenge to Christian orthodoxy. It also suggests some uneasiness on the part of its northern French author about the legitimacy of a northern French Crusade against their southern compatriots: although his influence was minimal in the south during the thirteenth century, technically the southerners were subjects of the French king just like their northern counterparts, and the idea of attacking fellow Frenchmen rather than Muslims may have worried some northerners. The comical, carnivalesque atmosphere of *Aucassin and Nicolette* deflects such anxieties into humor.

The other geographical pole of *Aucassin and Nicolette* is "Cartage" (section 36), which might refer either to Carthage, as I translate it, or to the Spanish port of Cartagena, both Muslim (or "Saracen," to use the *chantefable*'s medieval Christian designation) strongholds in the thirteenth century. For a thirteenth-century French audience, this Muslim/Saracen connection might suggest real-world anxieties too. The debacle of the Fourth Crusade, in which the Crusaders wound up slaughtering other Christians in Constantinople rather than Saracens, had taken place only shortly before the composition of *Aucassin and Nicolette*. The chronicles of Villehardouin[15] and of Robert de Clari,[16] which detail the Crusaders' activities in Constantinople, are roughly contemporary with *Aucassin and Nicolette*, and suggest another instance in which the concepts of Self and Other turned out to be difficult to disentangle: are other Christians also to be considered enemies like the Saracens? This Self/Other confusion is reflected in our hero's and heroine's names: Aucassin's name, though he is a Christian European, is derived from the Arabic language, while Nicolette's, though she is a "Saracen" by birth, is derived from a Christian saint—though we might also observe that while Nicolette's name seems French, it in fact derives from Asia Minor, making the lovers' exchange of identities perhaps less tidy than it seems to some observers.[17] Even the Saracen Other was thus not necessarily that different from the French Self in the thirteenth century, as María Rosa Menocal points out in her work on medieval Arabic-European cultural exchange: "In so markedly alluding to the difficulty of distinguishing Arab from French, in both name and origin, in so unmistakably pointing to the impossibility of clear-cut absolutes, *Aucassin et Nicolette* …is in fact placing itself squarely in the midst of the most vibrant and consequential Self-Other conflict of its day."[18] The early thirteenth century, in other words, witnessed events in which the very categories of Self and Other seemed to be dissolving. We may see *Aucassin and Nicolette* as working out in comic, poetic discourse the same issues of identity and otherness being pursued militarily in the Fourth and Albigensian Crusades, and elsewhere in thirteenth-century French culture.

GENDER, RACE, RELIGION, AND CLASS

These Self/Other relations are further complicated by considerations of gender, race, religion, and class. As we have seen, conventional medieval gender distinctions are to some extent reversed in *Aucassin and Nicolette*, with Nicolette generally playing the more active, adventurous role, while Aucassin for the most part passively waits for her to act. Nicolette, in addition to her stereotypically masculine activity, is also literally, if briefly, a cross-dresser, in the episode late in the story in which she disguises herself as a *jongleur* in order to escape from Cartagena/Carthage (sections 38–40). But Nicolette is a boundary-crosser in other ways, too: if her gender identity oscillates between masculine and feminine, her class and ethno-religious identities are unstable as well. She appears at various points in the story as a slave, a *jongleur* in the cross-dressing episode, and a princess in "Cartage"; she also oscillates between Christian and "Saracen" or Muslim/Arabic identities.

All of Nicolette's boundary crossings are related. Her characteristic adventurousness, for instance—her ability to perform traditionally "masculine" activities—might be linked in the Middle Ages to her ethnic and religious identities through the literary figure of "la belle Sarrasine," the "beautiful Saracen woman" who, as an exotic Other to western European, Christian femininity, was sometimes depicted as capable of performing seemingly masculine feats of valor.[19]

Her ethnic, religious, and gender identities are also linked to class. In "Cartage," Nicolette is identified as the king's daughter (section 38), and in Torelore, as we have seen, she could also be a princess; but, as is emphasized throughout the early Beaucaire sections, in Western Europe she is a slave, chattel bought and paid for by her godfather the viscount (sections 2, 4). *Aucassin and Nicolette*, indeed, for all its comic effects, is surprisingly accurate in its depiction of medieval slavery. Though slavery was in decline in the thirteenth century, the enslavement of Muslim captives was still fairly common in southern France,[20] where Beaucaire is located.

Nicolette's experience as a slave also had real-life counterparts in that female slaves might raise their social status through marriage,[21] as Nicolette does at the end of her story (section 41). It is worth noting that although his parents worry that Aucassin wishes to marry her (section 3), he himself never directly expresses such a desire until the very end, after her status as princess has been revealed (though in section 2, his use of the term "doner," which means either "to give" or "to give in marriage," might imply that he wishes to marry her). Throughout, he thinks of her more explicitly in terms of concubinage than of marriage: when the viscount warns him that keeping Nicolette as a concubine will lead him to Hell, for instance, Aucassin does not protest that his intentions are honorable, but responds only with the speech noted above, in which he declares that he would rather go to Hell anyway (section 6). Later, as Nicolette plans her escape from Beaucaire, Aucassin worries not that he will now be unable to marry her, but that someone else might make her his concubine (section 14). As a potential concubine, Nicolette again conforms to the reality of many female Muslim slaves' experience in medieval Europe; as a potential wife, she conforms to possibilities open to only a few.

"Race" in a more modern sense, that of skin color, plays its role in *Aucassin and Nicolette* as well. The whiteness of Nicolette's skin is emphasized throughout (as in section 12)—perhaps surprisingly, given that "Saracens" are routinely described in medieval literature as dark-skinned. But Nicolette has been baptized a Christian, as the count and viscount note more than once (sections 2 and 4), and medieval literature provides several examples in which Christian baptism turns dark "Saracen" skin white.[22] In this connection, we might note that when she is returned to "Cartage," Nicolette's father and brothers fail to recognize her as a fellow "Saracen": is her whiteness perhaps to be regarded as a recently acquired sign of baptism? Jacqueline de Weever has suggested that when Nicolette darkens her skin as part of her *jongleur* disguise in order to return to France, it is "a way of claiming her cultural inheritance for a brief period."[23] De Weever also points out that the term used for this darkening of the skin and its re-whitening on her return is "oinst," or "anoint" in English[24]; perhaps we might see these anointings symbolically as an un-baptism and a re-baptism.

Finally, it is worth pointing out that the name of the besieger of Beaucaire in the opening sections, Bougar de Valence, suggests the Old French terms "bogre" and "bougeron," both of which refer simultaneously to heresy and to sodomy, which were linked imaginatively in the medieval Christian mentality. Bougar thus perhaps raises the specter of several conscious or unconscious anxieties at once: military, sexual, and religious.

Race, religion, class, gender, and even sexuality are therefore inseparable categories in *Aucassin and Nicolette*. The *chantefable* anticipates, in a medieval comic mode, some of the most troubling issues confronted in modern and postmodern culture.

About This Edition and Translation

The manuscript of *Aucassin and Nicolette*, B.N. fonds français 2168, though somewhat difficult to read because of its relatively small size, cramped writing, and heavy (and sometimes eccentric) use of abbreviations, preserves a highly accurate text with little need of correction or emendation; where it is faulty, the correct readings are usually obvious. My edition, like most modern ones, is thus conservative. A photographic facsimile edition was produced by F. W. Bourdillon in 1896 (see note 2); because the original manuscript has undergone further deterioration in the intervening decades, the facsimile and its accompanying transcription are in some cases now preferable as a source. I have consulted both the manuscript and the facsimile in preparing the present edition. I have also consulted the editions of Mario Roques and of Jean Dufournet. Like many of my predecessors, I accept Hermann Suchier's conjectural emendations for those portions of the manuscript that were damaged before the preparation of the facsimile. All such corrections and emendations are indicated in the "Notes to the Old French Text." Punctuation has been brought into conformity with modern American English usage, and all abbreviations have been silently expanded.

The verse portions of the translation, in rhyming four-stress lines, aim to imitate the sense and spirit of the originals, rather than providing strict word-for-word equivalence; the prose sections strive for accuracy without archaism. The "Explanatory Notes to the English Translation" concern medieval terms or concepts that seem likely to be unfamiliar to modern students. In the interest of readability, I have kept such notes to a minimum.

NOTES

1. "Aucassin," the unheroic hero's name, is pronounced oh-cah-SAN.
2. The full contents are listed in the introduction to F. W. Bourdillon's facsimile edition, *Cest dAucasī & de Nicolete* (Oxford: Clarendon, 1896), 10–11. See also James R. Simpson, "Aucassin, Gauvain, and (Re)Ordering Paris, BNF, Fr. 2168," *French Studies* 66, no. 4 (2012): 451–66.
3. See Edelgard DuBruck, "The Audience of *Aucassin et Nicolete*: Confidant, Accomplice and Judge of Its Author," *Michigan Academician* 5, no. 2 (1972): 193–201.
4. For more examples, see *Prosimetrum: Crosscultural Perspectives in Prose and Verse*, ed. Karl Reichl and Joseph Harris (Woodbridge, Suffolk: D. S. Brewer, 1997); specifically on *Aucassin and Nicolette*, see Ardis Butterfield's contribution to *Prosimetrum*, "*Aucassin et Nicolette* and Mixed Forms in Medieval French," 67–98.
5. Bourdillon, ed., *Cest dAucasī & de Nicolete*. Butterfield, "Mixed Forms," transcribes the music in modern notation, p. 72.
6. Grace Frank, *The Medieval French Drama* (Oxford: Clarendon, 1954), 237.
7. Sarah Kay, "Genre, Parody, and Spectacle in *Aucassin et Nicolette* and Other Short Comic Tales," in *The Cambridge Companion to Medieval French Literature*, ed. Simon Gaunt and Sarah Kay (Cambridge: Cambridge University Press, 2008), 167–80. See also Omer Jodogne, "La Parodie et le pastiche dans 'Aucassin et

Nicolette,'" *Cahiers de l'Association Internationale des Études Françaises* 12 (1960): 53–65. Other critics have regarded the parodic element as more limited: see Tony Hunt, "La Parodie médiévale: Le cas d'*Aucassin et Nicolette*," *Romania* 100 (1979): 341–81; Imre Szabics, "Amour et prouesse dans *Aucassin et Nicolette*," in *Et c'est la fin pour quoi sommes ensemble: Hommage à Jean Dufournet*, ed. Jean-Claude Aubailly et al. (Paris: Champion, 1993), 1341–49; Mariantonia Liborio, "*Aucassin et Nicolette*: I limiti di una parodia," *Cultura neolatina* 30 (1970): 156–71.

8. For a more complete discussion of *Aucassin and Nicolette* as a parody of the *chanson de geste*, see Louisa Taha-Abdelghany, "*Aucassin et Nicolette* comme parodie de la chanson de geste," *Romance Review* 4, no. 1 (Spring 1994): 95–102.

9. Caroline A. Jewers, *Chivalric Fiction and the History of the Novel* (Gainesville: University Press of Florida, 2000), 45.

10. Norris J. Lacy, "Courtliness and Comedy in *Aucassin et Nicolette*," in *Essays in Early French Literature Presented to Barbara M. Craig*, ed. Norris J. Lacy and Jerry C. Nash (York, SC: French Literature Publications Company, 1982), 65–72, at 65.

11. On the theme of the "world upside down," see Moses Musonda, "Le Thème du 'monde à l'envers' dans *Aucassin et Nicolette*," *Medioevo romanzo* 7 (1981): 22–36.

12. See John Block Friedman, *The Monstrous Races in Medieval Art and Thought* (1982; repr. Syracuse: Syracuse University Press, 2000).

13. See Robert Griffin, "*Aucassin et Nicolette* and the Albigensian Crusade," *Modern Language Quarterly* 26 (1965): 243–56.

14. For a concise account of these events, see Mark Gregory Pegg, *The Corruption of Angels: The Great Inquisition of 1245–1246* (Princeton, NJ: Princeton University Press, 2001), 4; and for the role of Beaucaire in the Albigensian Crusade more broadly, Mark Gregory Pegg, *A Most Holy War: The Albigensian Crusade and the Battle for Christendom* (Oxford: Oxford University Press, 2008), 3–5, 150–52. *A Most Holy War* is an up-to-date account of the Crusade as a whole.

15. Geoffroy de Villehardouin, *La Conquête de Constantinople*, ed. Natalis de Wally, 3rd ed. (Paris: Firmin-Didot, 1882); *The Conquest of Constantinople*, in *Chronicles of the Crusades*, trans. M. R. B. Shaw (Harmondsworth, UK: Penguin, 1963), 29–160.

16. Robert de Clari, *La Conquête de Constantinople*, ed. Philippe Lauer (Paris: Champion, 1924); *The Conquest of Constantinople*, trans. Edgar Holmes McNeal (1936; repr. New York: Norton, 1969).

17. Joan B. Williamson, "Naming as a Source of Irony in 'Aucassin et Nicolette,'" *Studi Francesi*, n.s., 17 (1973): 401–9, at 401–2.

18. María Rosa Menocal, "Signs of the Times: Self, Other, and History in *Aucassin et Nicolette*," *Romanic Review* 80 (1989): 497–511, at 509.

19. On the figure of "la belle Sarrasine," see Jane Gilbert, "The Practice of Gender in *Aucassin et Nicolette*," *Forum for Modern Language Studies* 33, no. 3 (1997): 217–28, at 222–25.

20. See William D. Phillips, *Slavery from Roman Times to the Early Transatlantic Trade* (Minneapolis: University of Minnesota Press, 1985), 97–113; Jacques Heers, *Esclaves et domestiques au Moyen Âge dans le monde méditerranéen* (Paris: Fayard, 1981), 24, 26. See also Marc Bloch, "Personal Liberty and Servitude in the Middle Ages, Particularly in France: Contribution to a Class Study," in *Slavery and Serfdom in the Middle Ages*, trans. William R. Beer (Berkeley: University of California Press, 1975), 33–91, at 64.

21. Phillips, *Slavery*, 99, 102.

22. For several examples, see Thomas Hahn, "The Difference the Middle Ages Makes: Color and Race before the Modern World," *Journal of Medieval and Early Modern Studies* 31, no. 1 (2001): 1–37.

23. Jacqueline de Weever, "Nicolette's Blackness—Lost in Translation," *Romance Notes* 34 (1994): 317–25, at 322.

24. De Weever, "Nicolette's Blackness," 319.

par mout ensseres quant
ne le uerres. zseu eples zbos
peres le caun il adroiz
in z le enva lue zual mes
mes poirres auoir toute
piaz ce poere mex laue ar-
dese de iu delue coure dolas
Oz se cante

Aucasins si es cortois

li dolous zabes mes
damie ateus olen
ur nele puet coubrer
e meil bon coubsel don
er s le puluis es ales
len mairra les de gres
et ene ambre es eurst
romnea a ploter
z damie ame grecel
z fu dolade mrenes
us bege eluus
age ne nus zbege aleus
est dedurs z dous peulais
ge bordes zbege jouers
ge buitors bege acolers
oz chlir li adaler zbun
lauele me ne menel
z sene enre uel aler

Or dient
z content
Quer deuce amie zfablet
uerreus z aue. estou en
kambre z dre pretoir me
amiez le fut. bougeuis deul

lende zligns auoit asu
ur nesdublea mie. aue ar-
mande ses homes apue za
eual e sirele aucastel s
aller zhos lieue zlauest
zlicuable z zlebriant sa
ment. zseure ur al sier
zar mis por lcoustel desse
dre zsi borge il mentet
as aloours des murs. lis
cent enges z peus agresser
erueuens eluauis elboughs
zponers zleuis c. de ba
eure eune enluembre saut
fuldit deul z regre tait ni
tabe douce amie qtaut ame
hi sex saic el ques auer
z male ureux z truus don
asuer can castel toele uis
lez zlues fort zbaer sera
le peus q uiel deslue res
six eur pren les armes cun-
te seual zesen ce cure
zeuues ces homes z cuale
lba tan fiers sru home ni
aurel zsi teuient cus
sid sesderent il met les
auou zlor cois zte eque
zle muie zeu ues signs
zeslors q bieu se puet saure
zcaure le dous . pere cur
aue: en feler uous cor
ladex me mie luit neus
seledi mem fu ore ehole
neinem e eleual neuese
en ehor tan zebere chest
ne auers mie se uos ne me

Aucassin

and

Nicolette

C'est d'Aucasin et de Nicolete

This is about Aucassin and Nicolette

Qui[1] vauroit bons vers oïr

del deport du viel antif

de deus biax enfans petis,

Nicholete et Aucassins,

des grans paines qu'il soufri,

et des proueces qu'il fist,

por s'amie o le cler vis?

Dox est li cans, biax li dis[2]

Et cortois et bien asis:

nus hom n'est si esbahis,

tant dolans ni entrepris,

de grant mal amaladis,

se il l'oit, ne soit garis

et de joie resbaudis,

tant par est douce.

Who would like to lend their ears

to lines by a fellow old in years,[1]

written to please himself, with flair,

about a young, good-looking pair,[2]

Nicolette and Aucassin,[3]

the pains endured by this young man,

the deeds he did because he'd set

his heart on shining Nicolette?

The song is sweet, the tale is fine,

elegant in every line.

No one is so far depressed,

so sick, so sad, so short of zest,

who won't find healing in this tale,

and feel refreshed—it cannot fail—

that's how sweet it[4] is!

Or dient et content et fablent
que li quens Bougars de Valence faisoit guere au conte Garin de Biaucaire si grande et si mervelleuse et si mortel qu'il ne fust uns seus jors ajornés qu'il ne fust as portes et as murs et as bares de le vile a cent cevaliers et a dis mile sergens a pié et a ceval, si li argoit sa terre et gastoit son païs et ocioit ses homes.

Li quens Garins de Biaucaire estoit vix et frales, si avoit son tans trespassé. Il n'avoit nul oir, ne fil ne fille, fors un seul vallet. Cil estoit tex con je vos dirai.

Aucasins avoit a non li damoisiax. Biax estoit et gens et grans et bien taillés de ganbes et de piés et de cors et de bras. Il avoit les caviax blons et menus recercelés et les ex vairs et rians et le face clere et traitice et le nes haut et bien assis. Et si estoit enteciés de bones teces qu'en lui n'en avoit nule mauvaise se bone non. Mais si estoit soupris d'Amor, qui tout vaint, qu'il ne voloit estre cevalers, ne les armes prendre, n'aler au tornoi, ne fare point de quanque il deust.

Ses pere et se mere li disoient:

"Fix, car pren tes armes, si monte el ceval, si deffent te terre et aïe tes homes: s'il te voient entr'ex, si defenderont il mix lor cors et lor avoirs et te tere et le miue."

"Pere," fait Aucassins, "qu'en parlés vos ore? Ja Dix ne me doinst riens que je li demant, quant ere cevaliers, ne monte a ceval, ne que voise a estor ne a bataille, la u je fiere cevalier ni autres mi, se vos ne me donés Nicholete me douce amie que je tant aim."

"Fix," fait li peres, "ce ne poroit estre. Nicolete laise ester, que ce est une caitive qui fu amenee d'estrange terre, si l'acata li visquens de ceste vile as Sarasins, si l'amena en ceste vile, si l'a levee et bautisie et faite sa fillole, si li donra un de ces jors un baceler qui du pain li gaaignera par honor: de ce n'as tu que faire. Et se tu fenme vix avoir, je te donrai le file a un rai[1] u a un conte: il n'a si rice home en France, se tu vix sa fille avoir, que tu ne l'aies."

"Avoi, peres," fait Aucassins, "ou est ore si haute honers en terre, se Nicolete ma tresdouce amie l'avoit, qu'ele ne fust bien enploiie en li? S'ele estoit enpereris de Colstentinoble u d'Alemaigne, u roine de France u d'Engletere, si aroit il assés peu en li, tant est france et cortoise et de bon aire et entecie de toutes bones teces."

ℕow they speak and tell and recount[1]
that Count Bougar of Valence[2] was making mortal war on Count Garin of Beaucaire,[3] such a great and astonishing war that not a single day went by without his showing up outside the gates and walls and defenses of the city with a hundred knights and ten thousand mercenary soldiers,[4] on foot and on horse; and he burned Garin's lands and laid waste to his countryside and killed his men.

Count Garin of Beaucaire was old and frail, and had lived out his years; he had no heir, neither son nor daughter, except for one young gentleman.[5] I'll tell you what he was like.

This young nobleman was named Aucassin. He was tall and handsome and courtly, with well-formed legs and feet and body and arms. He had tightly curled blond hair and bright, laughing eyes and a shining, oval face with a proud and well-placed nose. And he was endowed with so many good qualities that there was no room left in him for any faults—but he was so unmanned by love, which conquers all, that he did not wish to be a knight or take up arms or go to tournaments or do anything he was supposed to do.

His father and mother said to him:

"Son, now put on your armor and get on your horse and defend your country and help your people. When they see you in their midst, they will be better able to defend themselves and their property—and your land and mine."

"Father," said Aucassin, "Now what are you talking about? Should I become a knight, may God give me nothing I ask for if I agree to mount a horse or to go into battle or combat, where I'd strike knights and get hit back, unless you give me my sweet love Nicolette, whom I love so much."

"Son," said his father, "that's not going to happen. Leave Nicolette be, for she's a captive who was brought here from foreign parts and whom the viscount of this city bought from the Saracens, brought to this city, raised and baptized and made his goddaughter. And one of these days he'll marry her off to some young gentleman[6] who will honorably earn her bread. It's got nothing to do with you. But if you want a wife, I'll get you the daughter of a king or a count; there's no man in France so prominent that you couldn't have his daughter, if you wanted her."

"Go on, father," said Aucassin. "Now where on earth is there any honor so great that it wouldn't suit Nicolette? If she were the empress of Constantinople or of Germany, or the queen of France or England, it still wouldn't be good enough for her—that's how generous, noble, and courteous she is, and endowed with all good qualities."

Or se cante.

Aucassins fu de Biaucaire,

d'un castel de bel repaire.

De Nicole le bien faite

nuis hom ne l'en puet retraire,

que ses peres ne l'i laisse

et sa mere le manace:

"Di va! faus, que vex tu faire?

Nicolete est cointe et gaie;[1]

jetee fu de Cartage,

acatee fu d'un Saisne.

Puis qu'a moullié te vix traire,

prem femme[2] de haut parage."

"Mere, je n'en puis el faire:

Nicolete est de boin aire;

ses gens cors et son viaire,

sa biautés le cuer m'esclaire.[3]

Bien est drois que s'amor aie,

que trop est douc."

Now it is sung.

Aucassin was from Beaucaire,

a peaceful castle, fine and fair.

No one could take his love away

from fair Nicole, whatever they'd say.

His father wouldn't let it be,[1]

his mother threatened warningly:

"What are you thinking, madman? Speak!

Nicolette is gay and chic,

but from Carthage[2] she was brought,

and from Saracens[3] was bought.

If you wish to take a wife,

choose her from our walk of life."

"Mother, I can't do otherwise:

Nicole is noble, fair, and wise;

her face, her body, every part—

her beauty heals my aching heart.

To have her love is right and smart:

that's how sweet she is!"

Or dient et content et flablent.

Quant li quens Garins de Biaucare vit qu'il ne poroit Aucassin son fil retraire des amors Nicolete, il traist au visconte de le vile qui ses hon estoit, si l'apela:

"Sire quens, car ostés Nicolete vostre filole! Que la tere soit maleoite dont ele fu amenee en cest païs! C'or par li pert jou Aucassin, qu'il ne veut estre cevaliers, ne faire point de quanque faire doie; et saciés bien que, se je le puis avoir,[1] que je l'arderai en un fu, et vous meismes porés avoir de vos tote peor."

"Sire," fait li visquens, "ce poise moi qu'il i va ne qu'il i vient ne qu'il i parole. Je l'avoie acatee de mes deniers, si l'avoie levee et bautisie et faite ma filole, si li donasse un baceler qui du pain li gaegnast par honor: de ce n'eust Aucassins vos fix que faire. Mais puis que vostre volentés est et vos bons, je l'envoierai en tel tere et en tel païs que ja mais ne le verra de ses ex."

"Or[2] gardés vous!" fait li quens Garins: "grans maus vos en porroit venir."

Il se departent. Et li visquens estoit molt rices hom, si avoit un rice palais par devers un gardin. En une canbre la fist metre Nicolete en un haut estage et une vielle aveuc li por conpagnie et por soisté tenir, et s'i fist metre pain et car et vin et quanque mestiers lor fu. Puis si fist l'uis seeler c'on n'i peust de nule part entrer ne iscir, fors tant qu'il i avoit une fenestre par devers le gardin assés petite dont il lor venoit un peu d'essor.

ℕow they speak and tell and recount.

When Count Garin of Beaucaire saw that he could not restrain his son Aucassin from loving Nicolette, he went to the city's viscount, who was his vassal, and demanded of him:

"Sir Count, send your goddaughter Nicolette away! A curse on the country from which she was brought here! For now because of her I am losing Aucassin, who does not wish to be a knight or to do anything else he's supposed to do. And understand this: if I could catch her, I'd burn her at the stake; and you should also fear for your own life."

"Sire," said the viscount, "it's a burden to me that Aucassin is always coming and going and talking with her. I bought her with my own money, raised her and baptized her and made her my goddaughter, and I'd like to give her to some young fellow who could honorably earn her bread; it shouldn't have anything to do with your son Aucassin. But, because you wish it and because it's for your good, I'll send her away to such a distant land and country that he'll never lay eyes on her again."

"Now make sure you do!" said Count Garin, "or she might bring you great misfortune."

They parted. And the viscount was a very rich man, and had a rich palace giving onto a garden. He had Nicolette put into a chamber on a high floor, with an old woman to keep her company and share her society, and he had bread, meat, wine, and other necessaries brought to them. Then he had the chamber door sealed so that no one could get in or out from any direction, except that there was a tiny window overlooking the garden, through which a little air came to them.

5

Or se cante.

Nicole est en prison mise

en une canbre vautie[1]

ki faite est par grant devisse,

panturee a miramie.

A la fenestre marbrine

la s'apoia la mescine.

Ele avoit blonde la crigne

et bien faite la sorcille,

la face clere et traitice:

ainc plus bele ne veïstes.

Esgarda par le gaudine,

et vit la rose espanie

et les oisax qui se crient,

dont se clama orphenine:

"Ai mi! lasse moi caitive!

por coi sui en prison misse?

Aucassins, damoisiax sire,

ja sui jou li vostre amie

et vos ne me haés mie!

Por vos sui en prison misse

en ceste canbre vautie

u je trai molt male vie.

Mais, par Diu le fil Marie,

longement n'i[2] serai mie,

se jel puis far."

Now it is sung.

A beautifully painted, vaulted[1] room,

cleverly made: it's Nicolette's doom

to be a wretched captive there.

The pretty girl with golden hair

(you've never seen anyone so rare),

with lovely brow and shining eye,

leans on the marble sill to sigh,

viewing the garden, about her woes.

Looking down at a flowering rose,

and hearing the birds, she declared that she

was an orphan. "Woe, oh woe is me!

Imprisoned in this barbican!

Hear me, young lord Aucassin:

I am still your own true love!

You like me, too, by God above.

I'm here detained because of you,

and life's unhappy. Still, it's true,

by Mary's son, I'll get to you—

if only I can do it!"

6

Or dient et content et fablent.

Nicolete[1] fu en prison, si que vous avés oï et entendu, en le canbre. Li cris et le noise ala par tote le terre et par tot le païs que Nicolete estoit perdue: li auquant dient qu'ele est fuie fors de la terre, et li auquant dient que li quens Garins de Biaucaire l'a faite mordrir. Qui qu'en eust joie, Aucassins n'en fu mie liés, ains traist au visconte de la vile, si l'apela:

"Sire visquens, c'avés vos fait de Nicolete ma tresdouce amie, le riens en[2] tot le mont que je plus amoie? Avés le me vos tolue ne enblee? Saciés bien que, se je en muir, faide vous en sera demandee; et ce sera bien drois, que vos m'arés ocis a vos deus mains, car vos m'avés tolu la riens en cest mont que je plus amoie."

"Biax sire," fait li quens, "car laisciés ester. Nicolete est une caitive que j'amenai d'estrange tere, si l'acatai de mon avoir a Sarasins, si l'ai levee et bautisie et faite ma fillole, si l'ai nourie, si li donasce un de ces jors un baceler qui del pain li gaegnast par honor. De ce n'avés vos que faire. Mais prendés le fille a un roi u a un conte. Enseurquetot, que cuideriés vous avoir gaegnié, se vous l'aviés asognentee ne mise a vo lit? Mout i ariés peu conquis, car tos les jors du siecle en seroit vo arme en infer, qu'en paradis n'enterriés vos ja."

"En paradis qu'ai je a faire? Je n'i quier entrer, mais que j'aie Nicolete ma tresdouce amie que j'aim tant, c'en paradis ne vont fors tex gens con je vous dirai. Il i vont ci viel prestre et cil viel clop et cil manke qui tote jor et tote nuit cropent devant ces autex et en ces viés croutes,[3] et cil a ces viés capes ereses et a ces viés tatereles vestues, qui sont nu et decauc et estrumelé, qui moeurent de faim et de soi et de froit et de mesaises. Icil vont en paradis: aveuc ciax n'ai jou que faire. Mais en infer voil jou aler, car en infer vont li bel clerc, et li bel cevalier qui sont mort as tornois et as rices gueres, et li buen[4] sergant et li franc home: aveuc ciax voil jou aler. Et s'i vont les beles dames cortoises que eles ont deus amis ou trois avoc leur barons, et s'i va li ors et li argens et li vairs et li gris, et si i vont herpeor et jogleor et li roi del siecle: avoc ciax voil jou aler, mais que j'aie Nicolete ma tresdouce amie aveuc mi."

"Certes," fait li visquens, "por nient en parlerés, que ja mais ne le verrés; et se vos i parlés et vos peres le savoit, il arderoit et mi et li en un fu, et vos meismes porriés avoir toute paor."

"Ce poise moi," fait Aucassins; se se[5] depart del visconte dolans.

14

Now they speak and tell and recount. Nicolette was imprisoned in this room, as you have already heard and understood. The rumor was noised about throughout the land and over all the countryside that Nicolette was lost; some said that she had fled the country, others that Count Garin of Beaucaire had had her killed. Whoever else may have rejoiced at these rumors, Aucassin was not one bit happy, but went to see the viscount, and called out to him:

"My lord viscount, what have you done with my sweet love Nicolette, the creature I love most in the whole world? Have you taken her off and stolen her from me? You should know that if this kills me, you will be held accountable; and that will only be just, for you will have killed me with your own two hands, because you took from me the creature I love most in this world."

"Dear sir," said the viscount, "leave her be. Nicolette is a captive whom I brought from another country; I bought her from the Saracens with my own money, raised her and baptized her and made her my goddaughter; I brought her up, and one day I would have given her to some young gentleman who would honorably have earned her bread. This has nothing to do with you. Take yourself the daughter of a king or count instead. After all, what did you hope to have gained if you had made her your mistress and taken her into your bed? It wouldn't have been much of a conquest for you, because you would have gone to Hell eternally, and you'd never have gotten into Heaven."

"What do I care about Heaven? I don't care if I go there, as long as I have my sweet love Nicolette,[1] whom I love so much, because the only people who go to Heaven are the ones I'm going to tell you about now: the ones who go there are all these old priests and maimed people, who grovel all day and all night before these altars and in all these old crypts, and people wearing old, torn cloaks and dressed in old rags, who are naked and barefoot and threadbare, and who are dying of hunger and thirst and cold and discomfort. These are the ones who go to Heaven, and I don't want anything to do with them. Instead, I want to go to Hell, because in Hell are the handsome, clever men and handsome knights who have died in tournaments and fabulous wars, and the good soldiers and noblemen: I want to go with them. And the beautiful, courtly ladies go there too, who have two or three lovers along with their husbands,[2] and that's also where the gold and silver and different kinds of fur[3] go, and the harpists and minstrels[4] and the kings of this world: these are the ones I want to go with—as long as I could have my sweet love Nicolette with me."

"Of course," said the viscount, "you're wasting your breath, because you're never going to see her again; and if you do speak with her, and your father finds out, he'll burn her and me together at the same stake, and you should fear for your own life as well."

"That's depressing," said Aucassin. He sorrowfully left the viscount.

7

Or se cante.

Aucasins s'en est tornés,

molt dolans et abosmés:

de s'amie o le vis cler

nus ne le puet conforter

ne nul bon consel doner.

Vers le palais est alés,

il en monta les degrés,

en une canbre est entrés,

si comença a plorer

et grant dol a demener

et s'amie a regreter:

"Nicolete, biax esters,

biax venir et biax alers,

biax deduis et dous parlers,

biax borders et biax jouers,

biax baisiers, biax acolers,

por vos sui si adolés

et si malement menés

que je n'en cuit vis aler,

suer, douce amie."

16

Now it is sung.

Aucassin has now gone back,

sorrowing (alas, alack)

about his fresh-faced Nicolette.

From no one, nowhere, can he get

advice or aid or counsel, so

back to the palace he must go,

up the stairs up to a room on high.

Aucassin began to cry

and sorrow for his Nicolette.

Making moan, he voiced regret:

"Nicolette, divine at rest,

no matter where, in talk and jest,

in warm embrace, I miss you so,

I'm so depressed and feel so low,

without your love, my life is woe,

my sister, my sweet love."

8

O r dient et content et fablent.

Entreusque Aucassins estoit en le canbre et il regretoit Nicolete s'amie, li quens Bougars de Valence, qui sa guerre avoit a furnir, ne s'oublia mie, ains ot mandé ses homes a pié et a ceval, si traist au castel por asalir. Et li cris lieve et la noise, et li cevalier et li serjant s'arment et qeurent as portes et as murs por le castel desfendre, et li borgois montent as aleoirs des murs, si jetent quariax et peus aguisiés.

Entroeusque li asaus estoit grans et pleniers, et li quens Garins de Biacaire vint en la canbre u Aucassins faisoit deul et regretoit Nicolete sa tresdouce amie que tant amoit.

"Ha! fix," fait il, "con par es caitis et maleurox, que tu vois c'on asaut ton castel tot le mellor et le plus fort; et saces, se tu le pers, que tu es desiretés. Fix, car pren les armes et monte u ceval et defen te tere, et aiues tes homes et va a l'estor: ja n'i fieres tu home ni autres ti, s'il te voient entr'ax, si desfenderont il mix lor avoir et lor cors et te tere et le miue. Et tu ies si grans et si fors que bien le pués faire, et farre le dois."

"Pere," fait Aucassins, "qu'en parlés vous ore? Ja Dix ne me doinst riens que je li[1] demant, quant ere cevaliers, ne monte el ceval, ne voise en estor, la u je fiere cevalier ne autres mi, se vos ne me donés Nicolete me douce amie que je tant aim."

"Fix," dist li pere, "ce ne puet estre: ançois sosferoie jo que je feusse tous desiretés, et que je perdisse quanques g'ai que tu ja l'euses a mollier ni a espouse."

Il s'en torne; et quant Aucassins l'en voit aler, il le rapela:

"Peres," fait Aucassins, "venés avant: je vous ferai bons couvens."

"Et quex, biax fix?"

"Je prendrai les armes, s'irai a l'estor, par tex covens que, se Dix me ramaine sain et sauf, que vos me lairés Nicolete me douce amie tant veir que j'aie deus paroles u trois a li parlees et que je l'aie une seule fois baisie."

"Je l'otroi," fait li peres.

Il li creante et Aucassins fu lié.

Now they speak and tell and recount.

While Aucassin was in his room, grieving for his love Nicolette, Count Bougar of Valence, who had a war to conduct, was not neglecting it, but had assembled his knights and his footsoldiers and took himself to the castle to attack it. And battle cries were raised and the alarm was sounded, and the knights and soldiers armed themselves and ran to the gates and walls to defend the castle, and the citizens climbed up onto the pathway around the ramparts, and flung down bricks and sharp pikes.

When the great assault was in full progress, Count Garin of Beaucaire went into the room where Aucassin was grieving and making moan for his very sweet love Nicolette, whom he loved so much.

"Ah, son," said he, "you are a miserable coward, for you can see that they are attacking your best and strongest castle; you know that if you lose it, you have no inheritance. So, son, take up your arms and mount your horse and defend your land, help your men, and get into battle: even if you don't strike down any men or get struck by anyone, still, if your men see you among them, they will defend their property and their persons more forcefully, and your land and mine. And you're so big and strong that you could easily do this; plus, it's your duty."

"Father," said Aucassin, "what are you talking about now? May God never grant me anything I ask of him if I become a knight or get on a horse or go into battle to strike or be struck by other knights, unless you give me my sweet love Nicolette, whom I love so much."

"Son," said his father, "that's not going to happen; in fact, I'd rather be completely dispossessed and lose everything I have than that you should ever have her for your wife or spouse."

He turned to go; and when Aucassin saw him going, he called him back.

"Father," said Aucassin, "come back. I'll make a deal with you."

"What is it, dear son?"

"I'll take up my arms and go into battle on condition that, if God brings me back safe and sound, you will allow me to see my sweet love Nicolette long enough to speak two or three words with her and to give her one kiss."

"I agree," said his father.

He promised, and Aucassin was overjoyed.

9

Or se cante.

Aucassins ot du baisier

qu'il ara au repairier:

por cent mile mars d'or mier

ne le fesist on si lié.

Garnemens demanda ciers,

on li a aparelliés;

il vest un auberc dublier

et laça l'iaume en son cief,

çainst l'espee au poin d'or mier,

si monta sor son destrier

et prent l'escu et l'espiel;

regarda andex ses piés,

bien li sissent es[1] estriers:

a mervelle se tint ciers.

De s'amie li sovient,

s'esperona li[2] destrier,

il li cort molt volentiers;

tot droit a le porte enl vient

a la bataille.

20

Now it is sung.

On his return, our boy's been told,

he'll get a kiss. The purest gold,

a hundred thousand marks or more,

would please him less—he's off to war!

He had his finest armor sought:

his hauberk,[1] double mail, was brought.

He donned his helm, that valiant lord,

and then his golden-hilted sword,

and took his buckler[2] and his lance.

He climbed his horse and viewed the stance,

upon their stirrups, of his feet,

delighted that they looked so neat.

He liked his looks, and thought once more

of Nicolette, his paramour,

and spurred his horse, who didn't wait,

but gladly galloped out the gate

into the battle.

21

10

Or dient et content.

Aucassins[1] fu armés sor son ceval, si con vos avés oï et entendu. Dix! con li sist li escus au col et li hiaumes u cief et li renge de s'espee sor le senestre hance! Et li vallés fu grans et fors et biax et gens et bien fornis, et li cevaus sor quoi il sist rades et corans, et li vallés l'ot bien adrecié par mi la porte. Or ne quidiés vous qu'il pensast n'a bués n'a vaces n'a civres prendre, ne qu'il ferist cevalier ne autres lui. Nenil nient! Onques ne l'en sovint; ains pensa tant a Nicolete sa douce amie qu'il oublia ses resnes et quanques il dut faire. Et li cevax qui ot senti les esperons l'en porta par mi le presse, se se lance tres entre mi ses anemis. Et il getent les mains de toutes pars, si le prendent, si le dessaisisent de l'escu et de le lance, si l'en mannent tot estrousement pris, et aloient ja porparlant de quel mort il le[2] feroient[3] morir. Et quant Aucassins l'entendi,

"Ha! Dix," fait il, "douce creature! Sont çou mi anemi mortel qui ci me mainent et qui ja me cauperont le teste? Et puis que j'arai la teste caupee, ja mais ne parlerai a Nicolete me douce amie que je tant aim. Encor ai je ci une bone espee et siec sor bon destrir sejorné! Se or ne me deffent por li, onques Dix ne li aït se ja mais m'aime!"

Li vallés fu grans et fors, et li cevax so quoi il sist fu remuans. Et il mist le main a l'espee, si comence a ferir a[4] destre et a senestre et caupe hiaumes et naseus et puins et bras et fait un caple entor lui, autresi con li senglers quant li cien l'asalent en le forest, et qu'il lor abat dis cevaliers et navre set et qu'il se jete tot estroseement de le prese et qu'il s'en revient les galopiax ariere, s'espee en sa main.

Li quens Bougars de Valence oï dire c'on penderoit Aucassin son anemi, si venoit cele part; et Aucassins ne le mescoisi mie; il tint l'espee en la main, se le fiert par mi le hiaume si qu'i li enbare el cief. Il fu si estonés qu'il caï a terre, et Aucassins tent le main, si le prent et l'en mainne pris par le nasel del hiame et le rent a son pere.

"Pere," fait Aucassins, "ves ci vostre anemi qui tant vous a gerroié et mal fait. .xx. ans[5] ja dure ceste guerre; onques ne pot iestre acievee par home."

"Biax fix," fait li pere, "tes enfances devés vos faire, nient baer a folie."

$\mathcal{N}$ow they speak and recount.

Aucassin was armed and on his horse, as you have already heard and understood. God, how well the shield hanging from his neck and the helmet on his head and the baldric of his sword on his left side became him! And the lad was big and strong and good-looking and noble and well put together, and the horse on which he sat was fast and lively, and the young man had directed it through the middle of the gate. And don't think that he was planning to go round up bulls or cows or sheep, nor that he was going to strike any knights or get struck back. Not at all! He wouldn't dream of it; instead, he was thinking about his sweet love Nicolette so much that he forgot about his reins and everything that he was supposed to do. And his horse, feeling the spurs, brought him into the thick of the battle and flung itself right into the midst of his enemies. And they reached out their arms on all sides and grabbed him, seized his shield and lance, and took him away, bound as a prisoner, and went off with him, wondering what sort of death they would make him die. And when Aucassin understood this,

"Oh God!" he said, "Gentle creator! Are these my mortal enemies who are taking me away and who are about to cut my head off? And once my head is cut off, I'll never again be able to talk with my sweet love Nicolette, whom I love so much. But I still have a good sword and I'm mounted on a well-rested horse; now, if I don't defend myself for her sake, may God never come to her aid, if ever she should love me!"

The young man was big and strong, and the horse on which he was mounted was spirited. So he put hand to sword and started to strike out left and right, and cut through helmets and nose-guards and wrists and arms, and cut down a circle around himself as a boar does when the hounds are assailing it in the forest, so that he brought down ten knights and wounded seven others, and he forced his way out of the press and retired to the rear at a gallop, sword in hand.

Count Bougar of Valence, who had heard tell that they were going to hang his enemy Aucassin, was coming after him; and Aucassin didn't fail to recognize him, not at all. He took his sword in his hand and struck him on the helmet, so fiercely that he jammed it down over his head. He was so dazed that he dropped to the ground, and Aucassin reached out his hand and took him prisoner and led him away by the nose-guard of his helmet and handed him over to his father.

"Father," said Aucassin, "here's your enemy who has been making war on you for so long, and doing wrong. This war has been going on for twenty years, and no one else has ever been able to put an end to it."

"Dear son," said his father, "this is just the kind of exploit a young man like yourself ought to be doing, not chasing after foolishness."

"Pere," fait Aucassins, "ne m'alés mie sermonant, mais tenés moi mes covens."

"Ba! quex covens, biax fix?"

"Avoi! pere, avés les vos obliees? Par mon cief! qui que les oblit, je nes voil mie oblier, ains me tient molt au cuer. Enne m'eustes vos en covent que, quant je pris les armes et j'alai a l'estor, que, se Dix me ramenoit sain et sauf, que vos me lairiés Nicolete ma douce amie tant veir que j'aroie[6] parlé a li deus paroles ou trois? Et que je l'aroie une fois baisie m'eustes vos en covent? Et ce voil je que[7] que vos me tenés."

"Jo?" fait li peres; "ja Dix ne m'aït, quant ja covens vos en tenrai; et s'ele estoit ja ci, je l'arderoie en un fu, et vos meismes porriés avoir tote paor."

"Est ce tote la fins?" fait Aucassins.

"Si m'aït Dix," fait li peres, "oïl."

"Certes," fait Aucassins, "je[8] sui molt dolans quant hom de vostre eage ment. Quens de Valence," fait Aucassins, "je vos ai pris?"

"Sire, voire fait. Aioire?" fait li quens.

"Bailiés ça vostre main," fait[9] Aucassins.

"Sire, volentiers."

Il li met se main en la siue.

"Ce m'afiés vos," fait Aucassins, "que, a nul jor que vos aiés a vivre, ne porrés men pere faire honte ne destorbier de sen cors ne de sen avoir que vos ne li faciés."

"Sire, por Diu," fait il, "ne me gabés mie; mais metés moi a raençon: vos ne me sarés ja demander or ni argent, cevaus ne palefrois, ne vair ne gris, ciens ne oisiax, que je ne vos doinse."

"Coment?" fait Aucassins; "ene connissiés vos que je vos ai pris?"

"Sire, oie," fait li quens Borgars.

"Ja Dix ne m'aït," fait Aucassins, "se vos ne le m'afiés, se je ne vous fac ja cele teste voler."

"Enondu!" fait il, "je vous afie quanque il vous plaist."

Il li afie, et Aucassins le fait monter sor un ceval, et il monte sor un autre, si le conduist tant qu'il fu a sauveté.

"Father," said Aucassin, "don't go on preaching at me, just keep the promise you made me."

"Bah! What promise, dear son?"

"Oh, come on, father, have you forgotten it? By my head, whoever else might forget it, I never will, because I know it by heart. Didn't you promise me that if I took up my arms and went into battle, and if God brought me back safe and sound, you would let me see my sweet love Nicolette long enough to speak two or three words with her? And didn't you promise me that I could give her one kiss? And that's the promise I want you to keep."

"Me?" said his father, "May God never help me if I keep that promise; and if she were here, I'd burn her at the stake, and you might also fear for your own life."

"Is that your last word?" said Aucassin.

"So help me God," said his father, "yes."

"Well," said Aucassin, "I'm certainly very disappointed that a man of your age would lie. Count of Valence," said Aucassin, "I took you prisoner?"

"Yes, sir, that's true. So?" said the count.

"Put your hand here," said Aucassin.

"Gladly, sir."

25

He put his hand in Aucassin's.

"Swear to me," said Aucassin, "that you will never fail to try to shame my father and cause distress to his person and property, by whatever means, for the rest of your life."

"By God, sir," said he, "don't mock me, but put me up for ransom. You couldn't ask for anything that I wouldn't give: gold or silver, warhorse or palfrey,[1] or any kind of fur or dogs or birds."

"What?" said Aucassin. "Don't you agree that I have taken you prisoner?"

"Yes, sir," said Count Bougar of Valence.

"May God never help me," said Aucassin, "if I don't relieve you of your head unless you swear this oath."

"In God's name," said he, "I swear to do whatever you like."

He swore to him, and Aucassin had him mounted on a horse, and he mounted another himself, and escorted him to safety.

Or se cante.

Quant or voit li quens Garins

de son enfant Aucassin

qu'il ne pora departir

de Nicolete au cler vis,

en une prison l'a mis

en un celier sosterin

qui fu fais de marbre bis.

Quant or i vint Aucassins,

dolans fu, ainc ne fu si;

a dementer si se prist

si con vos porrés oïr:

"Nicolete, flors de lis,

douce amie o le cler vis,

plus es douce que roisins

ne que soupe en maserin.

L'autr' ier vi un pelerin,

nés estoit de Limosin,

malades de l'esvertin,

si gisoit ens en un lit,

mout par estoit entrepris,

de grant mal amaladis.

Tu passas devant son lit,

si soulevas ton traïn

et ton peliçon ermin,

la cemisse de blanc lin,

tant que ta ganbete vit:

*N*ow it is sung.

When his father, Count Garin,

saw that his child, Aucassin,

had his heart entirely set

upon the fresh-faced Nicolette,

in a marble crypt he found

a prison for him. Underground,

in darkness, our friend Aucassin,

on his arrival there, began

to mourn her loss. He'd never been

so sad in all his life. His keen

laments went thus, as you shall hear:

"Nicole, my lily, fresh-faced dear,

more sweet to me than bread in wine,

than grapes that come fresh off the vine,

I saw a man from Limousin

the other day," said Aucassin,

"a pilgrim groaning in his bed,

so ill that he was off his head,

so ill that he was nearly dead.

But when you passed his bed of pain,

and held your ermine tunic's train,

and linen shift, so fresh and white,

your pretty leg came into sight,

garis fu li pelerins

et tos sains, ainc ne fu si.

Si se leva de son lit,

si rala en son païs

sains et saus et tos garis.

Doce amie, flors de lis,

biax alers et biax venirs,

biax jouers et biax bordirs,

biax parlers et biax delis,

dox baisiers et dox sentirs,

nus ne vous poroit haïr.

Por vos sui en prison mis

en ce celier sousterin

u je fac mout male fin;

or m'i[1] convenra morir

por vos, amie."

and he was cured, jumped out of bed,
and went right home, high-spirited,
completely healed, as good as new.
My sweet, my love, my lily, you
are lovely in the way you walk
and lovely in our playful talk,
in hugs and kisses lovely too.
Who could keep from loving you?
For love of you I now am bound
here in this cellar underground,
and weep, and moan, and groan, and cry.
There's nothing left to do but die
for you, my love."

12

Or dient et content et fabloient.

Aucasins fu mis en prison, si com vos avés oï et entendu, et Nicolete fu d'autre part en le canbre. Ce fu el tans d'esté, el mois de mai que li jor sont caut, lonc et cler, et les nuis coies et series.

Nicolete jut une nuit en son lit, si vit la lune luire cler par une fenestre et si oï le lorseilnol center en garding, se li sovint d'Aucassin sen ami qu'ele tant amoit. Ele se comença a porpenser del[1] conte Garin de Biaucaire qui de mort le haoit, si se pensa qu'ele ne remanroit plus ilec, que, s'ele estoit acusee et li quens Garins le savoit, il le feroit de male mort morir. Ele senti que li vielle dormoit qui aveuc li estoit; ele se leva, si vesti un bliaut de drap de soie que ele avoit molt bon, si prist dras de lit et touailes, si noua l'un a l'autre, si fist une corde si longe conme ele pot, si le noua au piler de le fenestre; si s'avala contreval le gardin, et prist se vesture a l'une main devant et a l'autre deriere, si s'escorça por le rousee qu'ele vit grande sor l'erbe, si s'en ala aval le gardin.

Ele avoit les caviaus blons et menus recercelés, et les ex vairs et rians, et le face traitice, et le nés haut et bien assis, et lé levretes vremelletes plus que n'est cerisse ne rose el tans d'esté, et les dens blans et menus; et avoit les mameletes dures qui li souslevoient sa vesteure ausi con ce fuissent deus nois gauges; et estoit graille par mi les flans qu'en vos dex mains le peusciés enclorre; et les flors des margerites qu'ele ronpoit as ortex de ses piés, qui li gissoient sor le menuisse du pié par deseure, estoient droites noires avers ses piés et ses[2] ganbes, tant par estoit blance la mescinete.

Ele vint au postic, si le deffrema, si s'en isci par mi les rues de Biaucaire par devers l'onbre, car la lune luisoit molt clere, et erra tant qu'ele vint a le tor u ses amis estoit. Li tors estoit faelee de lius en lius; et ele se quatist delés l'un des pilers, si s'estraint en son mantel, si mist sen cief par mi une creveure de la tor qui vielle estoit et anciienne, si oï Aucassin qui la dedens plouroit et faisoit mot grant dol et regretoit se douce amie que tant amoit. Et quant el l'ot assés escouté, si comença a dire.

30

Now they speak and tell and recount.

Aucassin had been imprisoned, as you have already heard and understood, and Nicolette, for her part, was in her chamber. It was summertime, in the month of May, when the days are warm, long, and luminous, and the nights calm and serene.

One night as Nicolette lay in bed, she saw the moon shining brightly through her window and she heard the nightingale singing in the garden, and she thought back on her love Aucassin, whom she loved so much. She began to think about Count Garin of Beaucaire, who mortally hated her, and she decided she would remain in that place no longer, because, if someone made an accusation against her and Count Garin learned of it, he would cause her to die a painful death. She noticed that the old woman who was with her was asleep; she got up and put on a very fine silk tunic that she had, and took her bedclothes and towels and tied them all together and made a rope as long as she could and tied it to the window frame. She climbed down into the garden, and took hold of her dress with one hand in front and the other behind, and lifted it up because of the dew she saw lying heavily on the grass, and made her way to the end of the garden.

She had blond, tightly curled hair, lively, laughing eyes, an oval face, a high, well-placed nose, lips redder than a cherry or a rose in summertime, and small, white teeth; and she had firm little breasts pushing at her dress like two large walnuts; and she had such a slender figure that you could have encircled it with two hands; and the daisies that she broke and trampled under her feet as she walked were completely black compared with her feet and legs, so white was this girl.

She came to the postern gate, opened it, and went out into the streets of Beaucaire, keeping to the shadows, because the moon was shining so brightly, and went on until she came to the tower where her lover was. The tower was cracked in several places; and she hid behind a pillar and covered herself with her mantle, and put her head in at a crack in the tower, which was old and decrepit, and heard Aucassin inside, who was weeping and greatly sorrowing and pining for his sweet love whom he loved so much. And when she had heard enough, she began to speak.

13

Or se cante.

Nicolete o le vis cler

s'apoia a un piler,

s'oï Aucassin plourer

et s'amie a regreter;

or parla, dist son penser:

"Aucassins, gentix et ber,

frans damoisiax honorés,

que vos vaut li dementer,

li plaindres ne li plurers,

quant ja de moi ne gorés?

Car vostre peres me het

et trestos vos parentés.

Por vous passerai le mer,

s'irai en autre regnés."

De ses caviax a caupés,

la dedens les a rüés.

Aucassins les prist, li ber,

si les a molt honorés

et baisiés et acolés;

en sen sain les a boutés;

si recomence a plorer

tout por s'amie.

32

Now it is sung.

Nicolette, her face aglow,

by the pillar heard the woe

that weeping, grieving Aucassin

was making. Shortly she began

to speak of what was on her mind:

"Aucassin, so high and kind,

my lord, just what good can it do

to cry and mourn? I'm not for you.

Your noble father hates me so,

and all your family, I must go

away, for your sake—who knows where?"

Nicole has cut a lock of hair

and tossed it in to Aucassin.

He held it fast, that noble man,

embraced it, kissed it, let it lie

beside his heart—and began to cry

again, all for his love.

14

Or dient et content et fabloient.

Qant Aucassins oï dire Nicolete qu'ele s'en voloit aler en autre païs, en lui n'ot que courecier.

"Bele douce amie," fait il, "vos n'en irés mie, car dont m'ariis vos mort. Et li premiers qui vos verroit ne qui vous porroit, il vos prenderoit lués et vos meteroit a son lit, si vos asoignenteroit. Et puis que vos ariiés jut en lit a home, s'el mien non, or ne quidiés mie que j'atendisse tant que je trovasse coutel dont je me peusce ferir el cuer et ocirre. Naie voir, tant n'atenderoie je mie; ains m'esquelderoie de si lonc que je verroie une maisiere u une bisse pierre, s'i hurteroie si durement me teste que j'en feroie les ex voler et que je m'escerveleroie tos. Encor ameroie je mix a morir de si faite mort que je seusce que vos eusciés jut en lit a home, s'el mien non."

"A!" fait ele, "je ne quit mie que vous m'amés tant con vos dites; mais je vos aim plus que vos ne faciés mi."

"Avoi!" fait Aucassins, "bele douce amie, ce ne porroit estre que vos m'amissiés tant que je fac vos. Fenme ne puet tant amer l'oume con li hom fait le fenme; car li amors de le fenme est en son oeul et en son le cateron de sa mamele et en son l'orteil del pié, mais li amors de l'oume est ens el cué plantee, dont ele ne puet iscir."

34 La u Aucassins et Nicolete parloient ensanble, et les escargaites de le vile venoient tote une rue, s'avoient les espees traites desos les capes, car li quens Garins lor avoit conmandé que, se il le pooient prendre, qu'i l'ocesissent. Et li gaite qui estoit sor le tor les vit venir, et oï qu'il aloient de Nicolete parlant et qu'il le maneçoient a occirre.

"Dix!" fait il, "con grans damages de si bele mescinete, s'il l'ocient! Et molt seroit grans aumosne, se je li pooie dire, par quoi il ne s'aperceuscent, et qu'ele s'en gardast; car s'i l'ocient, dont iert Aucassins mes damoisiax mors, dont grans damages ert."

Now they speak and tell and recount.

When Aucassin heard Nicolette say that she intended to go to some other country, he felt only distress within.

"Fair sweet love," said he, "don't go, for you'd be killing me. And the first man who saw you and was able, would immediately take you into his bed and have his way with you. And as soon as you had slept in another man's bed—other than mine—don't think for a moment that I'd wait until I found a knife with which I could stab myself in the heart and kill myself. No, truly I wouldn't wait for any such thing, but as soon as I saw a wall or a block of granite, I'd fling and hurl my head against it so hard that I'd gouge out my eyes and dash out all my brains. In fact, I'd rather die such a death than learn that you had slept in some man's bed, other than mine."

"Ah," said she, "I don't really believe you love me as much as you claim; but I love you better than you love me."

"Go on!" said Aucassin, "fair sweet love, it's impossible that you could love me as much as I do you. A woman cannot love a man as the man does the woman, because a woman's love is in her eye and in the nipple of her breast and down as far as the toe of her foot, but the man's love is planted in his heart, from which it cannot depart."

While Aucassin and Nicolette were talking together, the city's archers were advancing along a street, and had their swords drawn beneath their capes, because Count Garin had commanded them to kill her if they could capture her. And the watchman who was on top of the tower saw them coming, and he heard them talking about Nicolette as they went along, and that they were threatening to kill her.

"God!" said he, "What a great loss it would be if they killed that beautiful girl! And it would be a great charity for me to warn her without their knowledge, and if she could be put on her guard; because if they kill her, then my young lord Aucassin would die, which would be a great loss."

15

Or se cante.

Li gaite fu mout vaillans,

preus et cortois et saçans.

Il a comencié un cant[1]

ki biax fu et avenans.

"Mescinete o le cuer franc,

cors as gent et avenant,

le poil blont et avenant,

vairs les ex, ciere rïant.

Bien le voi a ton sanblant:

parlé as a ton amant

qui por toi se va morant.

Jel te di et tu l'entens:

garde toi des souduians

ki par ci te vont querant,

sous les capes les nus brans;

forment te vont maneçant,

tost te feront messeant,

s'or ne t'i gardes."

36

Now it is sung.
The watchman was polite and brave
and clever, and he wished to save
Nicole, so he began to sing
a pretty song, inspiriting:
"You—young girl of noble heart,
with your figure sweet and smart,
hair that's blond, a look that's clear,
alive, and glad—it would appear
you've seen your lover in this place
(I see it clearly in your face),
who's nearly dead for love of you.
Listen now and hear a clue:
be on your guard against a few
faithless men who seek for you,
each with a sword beneath his cape,
warning that you won't escape
their malice: you'll be in a scrape,
if you're not on guard."

16

Or dient et content et fabloient.

"Hé!" fait Nicolete, "l'ame de ten pere et de te mere soit en benooit repos, quant si belement et si cortoisement le m'as ore dit. Se Diu plaist, je m'en garderai bien, et Dix m'en gart!"

Ele s'estraint en son mantel en l'onbre del piler, tant que cil furent passé outre; et ele prent congié a Aucassin, si s'en va tant qu'ele vint au mur del[1] castel. Li murs fu depeciés, s'estoit rehordés, et ele monta deseure, si fist tant qu'ele fu entre le mur et le fossé; et ele garda contreval, si vit le fossé molt parfont et molt roide, s'ot molt grant paor.

"Hé, Dix," fait ele,[2] "douce creature! Si je me lais caïr, je briserai le col, et se je remain ci, on me prendera demain, si m'arde on en un fu. Encor ainme je mix que je muire ci que tos li pules me regardast demain a merveilles."

Ele segna son cief, si se laissa glacier aval le fossé, et quant ele vint u fons, si bel pié et ses beles mains, qui n'avoient mie apris c'on les bleçast, furent quaissies et escorcies et li sans en sali bien en dose lius, et ne por quant ele ne santi ne mal ne dolor por le grant paor qu'ele avoit. Et se ele fu en paine de l'entrer, encor fu ele en forceur de l'iscir. Ele se pensa qu'ileuc ne faisoit mie bon demorer, et trova un pel aguisié que cil dedens avoient jeté por le castel deffendre, si fist pas un avant l'autre tant, si monta tant a grans painnes qu'ele vint deseure. Or estoit li forés pres a deus arbalestees, qui bien duroit trente liues de lonc et de lé, si i avoit bestes sauvages et serpentine. Ele ot paor que, s'ele i entroit, qu'eles ne l'ocesiscent, si se repensa que, s'on le trovoit ileuc, c'on le remenroit en le vile por ardoir.

Now they speak and tell and recount.

"Ah!" said Nicolette, "may your father's soul and your mother's live in blessed repose, now that you have warned me so nicely and nobly. God willing, I'll be on guard against them, and may God protect me!"

She covered herself with her cloak, in the shadow of the pillar, until they had passed. And she took her leave of Aucassin, and went on her way until she came to the castle wall. The wall was damaged and had been rebuilt, and she climbed up onto it, and moved along until she was between the wall and the moat, and she looked down and saw that the moat was very deep and steep, and she was very frightened.

"Ah, God," said she, "gentle being! If I let myself fall, I'll break my neck, and if I stay here, they will catch me tomorrow and burn me in a fire. Still, I'd rather die here than have everyone staring at me in amazement tomorrow."

She crossed herself on the forehead, and let herself slide into the moat, and when she touched the bottom, her pretty feet and her pretty hands, which had never before been wounded by anything, were bruised and scratched, and the blood flowed out in more than a dozen places, but nevertheless she felt no pain or hurt, because of her great fear. And if she had trouble getting in, she had even more getting out. She knew it wouldn't be a good idea to stay there, and found one of the sharp pikes that those inside had thrown down in order to defend the castle, and she put one foot in front of the other, and climbed with great difficulty until she came out on top. Now the forest was only two bowshots away, and it was full of wild beasts and serpents. She was afraid that if she went in there, they would kill her; but she thought that if she was found where she was, they would bring her back to the city to burn.

17

Or se cante.

Nicolete o le vis cler

fu montee le fossé,

si se prent a dementer

et Jhesum a reclamer:

"Peres, rois de maïsté,

or ne sai quel part aler:

se je vois u gaut ramé,

ja me mengeront li lé,

li lion et li sengler

dont il i a a[1] plenté;

et se j'atent le jor cler

que on me puist ci trover,

li fus sera alumés

dont mes cors iert enbrasés.

Mais, par Diu de maïsté,

encor aim jou mix assés[2]

que me mengucent li lé,

li lion et li sengler,

que je voisse en la cité:

je n'irai mie."

40

Now it is sung.

She climbed, did shining Nicolette,

outside the moat, but, still upset,

invoking Jesus' name, in woe,

said, "God, I don't know where to go.

O King majestic, kind, and good,

if I should go into the wood,

the wolf, the roaring lion, the boar,

of which there are many, and always more,

will eat me. But if I should wait

for daybreak, this will be my fate:

they'll find me and they'll light a pyre,

and burn my body up with fire.

By the God of majesty,

it seems a better fate to me

for wolves and boars to gulp me down,

and lions, than go back to town:

I won't go back at all!"

18

Or dient et content et fabloient.

Nicolete se dementa molt, si con vos avés oï. Ele se conmanda a Diu, si erra tant qu'ele vint en le forest. Ele n'osa mie parfont entrer por les bestes sauvaces et por le serpentine, si se quatist en un espés buisson; et soumax li prist, si s'endormi dusqu'au demain a haute prime que li pastorel iscirent de la vile et jeterent lor bestes entre le bos et la riviere, si se traien d'une part a une molt bele fontaine qui estoit au cief de la forest, si estendirent une cape, se missent lor pain sus. Entreusque il¹ mengoient, et Nicolete s'esveille au cri des oisiax et des pastoriax, si s'enbati sor aus.

"Bel enfant," fait ele,² "Damedix vos i aït!"

"Dix vos benie!" fait li uns qui plus fu enparlés des autres.

"Bel enfant," fait ele,³ "conissiés vos Aucassin, le fil le conte Garin de Biaucaire?"

"Oïl, bien le counisçons nos."

"Se Dix vos aït, bel enfant," fait ele, "dites li qu'il a⁴ une beste en ceste forest et qu'i le viegne cacier, et s'il l'i puet prendre, il n'en donroit mie un menbre por cent mars d'or, non por cinc cens, ne por nul avoir."

Et cil le regardent, se le virent si bele qu'il en furent tot esmari.

"Je li dirai?" fait cil qui plus fu enparlés des autres; "dehait ait qui ja en parlera, ne qui ja li dira! C'est fantosmes que vos dites, qu'il n'a si ciere beste en ceste forest, ne cerf, ne lion, ne sengler, dont uns des menbres vaille plus de dex deniers u de trois au plus, et vos parlés de si grant avoir! Ma dehait qui vos en croit, ne qui ja li dira! Vos estes fee, si n'avons cure de vo conpaignie, mais tenés vostre voie."

"Ha! bel enfant," fait ele, "si ferés. Le beste a tel mecine que Aucassins ert garis de son mehaing; et j'ai ci cinc sous en me borse: tenés, se li dites; et dedens trois jors li covient cacier, et se il dens trois jors ne le trove, ja mais n'iert garis de son mehaig."

"Par foi," fait il, "les deniers prenderons nos, et s'il vient ci, nos li dirons, mais nos ne l'irons ja quere."

"De par Diu!" fait ele.

Lor prent congié as pastoriaus, si s'en va.

Now they speak and tell and recount.

Nicolette was most unhappy, as you have heard. She commended herself to God, and went on her way until she came to the forest. She didn't dare enter too deeply into it, because of the wild animals and serpents, so she hid in a thick bush; and sleep overtook her, and she slept until past the hour of prime[1] the following day, when the shepherds were coming out of the city and driving their beasts between the woods and the river. They went off in the direction of a very pretty spring at the edge of the forest, and spread out a cloak, and set out their meal on it. While they were eating, Nicolette awakened to the voices of the birds and the little shepherd boys, and she hastened up to them.

"Dear children," said she, "may God aid you!"

"God bless you!" said the first, who was better-spoken than the others.

"Dear children," said she, "do you know Aucassin, the son of Count Garin of Beaucaire?"

"Yes, we know him well."

"So help you God, dear children," said she, "tell him that there's a beast in the woods and that he should come hunting it, because if he could catch it, he wouldn't sell a single one of its limbs for a hundred marks of gold, nor for five hundred, nor for any amount."

And they looked at her, and found her so beautiful that they were completely astonished.

"I'm to tell him that?" said the one who was better-spoken than the others. "May God hate whoever says this or speaks it! What you're saying is a fantasy, for there is no beast in this forest, neither deer nor lion nor boar, so precious that one of its limbs is worth more than two deniers, or three at most, and you're talking about such great wealth. May God hate whoever believes you and whoever says this! You're some fairy, and we don't want your company,[2] so be on your way!"

"Ah, pretty children," said she, "you will do this. This beast has such a medicine as will cure Aucassin of his ill health; and I have five sous in my purse: take them, and tell him; and he must start hunting within three days, for if he doesn't catch it in three days, he'll never be cured of what ails him."

"In faith," said he, "we'll take the coins, and if he comes by, we'll tell him, but we won't go looking for him."

"It's in God's hands!" said she.

Then she took her leave of the shepherds and went on her way.

43

Or se cante.

Nicolete o le cler vis
des pastoriaus se parti,
si acoilli son cemin[1]
tres par mi le gaut foilli
tout un viés sentier anti,
tant qu'a une voie vint
u aforkent set cemin
qui s'en vont par le païs.
A porpenser or se prist
qu'esprovera son ami
s'i l'aime si com il dist.
Ele prist des flors de lis
et de l'erbe du garris
et de le foille autresi;
une bele loge en fist:
ainques tant gente ne vi.
Jure Diu qui ne menti,
se par la vient Aucasins
et il por l'amor de li
ne s'i repose un petit,
ja ne[2] sera ses amis,
n'ele s'amie.

Now it is sung.

Lovely, bright-faced Nicolette

left the shepherd boys, and set

out upon her path, which lay

through the leafy woods. Her way

went all along an ancient track

until she took another tack:

she found a crossroads where she met

seven pathways. Nicolette,

at the crossing, thought she'd prove

the truth about her lover's love:

was it strong as he had said?

She gathered lilies from a bed

of native flowers there, in sheaves,

and added to them lots of leaves.

With these she built a bower green,

a prettier I've never seen.

She swore to God, who'd never lie,

that if her lover happened by,

and didn't pause to take his rest,

for love, here in this pretty nest,

he'd never love her—it's a test—

nor would she love him.

20

Or dient et content et fabloient.

Nicolete eut faite le loge, si con vos avés oï et entendu, molt bele et mout gente, si l'ot bien forree dehors et dedens de flors et de foilles, si se repost delés le loge en un espés buison por savoir que Aucassins feroit.

Et li cris et li noise ala par tote le tere et par tot le païs que Nicolete estoit perdue: li auquant dient qu'ele en estoit fuie, et li autre dient que li quens Garins l'a faite mordrir. Qui qu'en eust joie, Aucassins n'en fu mie liés. Et li quens Garins ses peres le fist metre hors de prison, si manda les cevaliers de le tere et les damoiseles, si fist faire une mot rice feste, por çou qu'il cuida Aucassin son fil conforter.

Quoi que li feste estoit plus plaine, et Aucassins fu apoiiés a une puie tos dolans et tos souples. Qui que demenast joie, Aucassins n'en ot talent, qu'il n'i veoit rien de çou qu'il amoit. Uns cevaliers le regarda, si vint a lui, si l'apela.

"Aucassins," fait il, "d'ausi fait mal con vos avés ai je esté malades. Je vos donrai bon consel, se vos me volés croire."

"Sire," fait Aucassins, "grans mercis; bon consel aroie je cier."

"Montés sor un ceval," fait il, "s'alés selonc cele forest esbanoiier; si verrés ces flors et ces herbes, s'orrés ces oisellons canter; par aventure orrés tel parole dont mix vos iert."

"Sire," fait Aucassins, "grans mercis; si ferai jou."

Il s'enble de la sale, s'avale les degrés, si vient[1] en l'estable ou ses cevaus estoit. Il fait metre le sele et le frain; il met pié en estrier, si monte, et ist del castel, et erra tant qu'il vint a le forest, et cevauca tant qu'il vint a le fontaine, et trove les pastoriax au point de none; s'avoient une cape estendue sor l'erbe, si mangoient lor pain et faisoient mout tresgrant joie.

46

$\mathcal{N}$ow they speak and tell and recount.
Nicolette had made her bower, as you have heard and understood, very beautiful and very pleasant, and had decorated it, outside and inside, with flowers and leaves, and she posted herself near the hut, in a thick bush, to see whether Aucassin would come.

And the gossip and rumor that Nicolette was missing spread all through the land and all through the countryside: some said she had fled, and others said that Count Garin had had her murdered. Whoever might have gotten pleasure from this news, Aucassin was not at all pleased about it. And Count Garin, his father, had him taken out of prison, and summoned the knights and damsels of his land and had a very grand feast prepared for them, because he thought it might console his son Aucassin.

While the festivities were at their height, Aucassin was leaning on a balustrade, all sorrowful and desolate. Whoever else might be enjoying themselves, Aucassin had no desire to do so, because he didn't see there the creature he loved. A knight was watching him, and came up and spoke to him:

"Aucassin," said he, "I myself have been sick with this same sickness you have. I'll give you some good advice, if you'll trust me."

"Sir," said Aucassin, "thank you very much. I value good advice."

"Get on your horse," said he, "and go distract yourself in the woods: you'll look at the flowers and plants; you'll listen to the birds singing; and maybe you'll hear something that will make you feel better."

"Sir," said Aucassin, "many thanks. I'll do it!"

He left the hall and descended the steps, and came to the stable where his horse was kept. He had the saddle and bridle put on; he put his foot in the stirrup, and mounted, and rode out of the castle, and he traveled until he came to the forest, and rode until he arrived at the spring, and found the shepherd boys just at none;[1] they had spread a cloak out on the grass, and were eating their bread and making great merriment.

21

Or se cante.

Or s'asanlent pastouret,

Esmerés et Martinés,

Früelins et Johanés,

Robeçons et Aubriés.

Li uns dist: "Bel conpaignet,

Dix aït Aucasinet,

voire a foi, le bel vallet;

et le mescine au corset[1]

qui avoit le poil blondet,

cler le vis et l'oeul vairet,

ki nos dona denerés

dont acatrons gastelés,

gaïnes et coutelés,

flaüsteles et cornés,

maçuëles et pipés,

Dix le garisse!"

Now it is sung.

The shepherds are assembled there,

Fruëlin, his friend Emere,

young Jeannot and Martinet,

Robichon and Aubriet.

One said, "Dearest company,

God save Aucassin, for he

is gentlemanly, young, and free;

the maiden also, dressed so fair,

fresh of face, with golden hair

and lively eye, who let us take

enough *deniers* to buy this cake,[1]

and knives and sheaths of different types,

and flutes and horns and clubs and pipes,

may God save her!"

49

22

Or dient et content et fabloient.

Quant Aucassins oï les pastoriax, si li sovint de Nicolete se tresdouce amie qu'il tant amoit, et si se pensa qu'ele avoit la esté. Et il hurte le ceval des eperons, si vint as pastoriax.

"Bel enfant, Dix vos i aït!"

"Dix vos benie!" fait cil qui fu plus enparlés des autres.

"Bel enfant," fait il, "redites le cançon que vos disiés ore!"

"Nous n'i dirons," fait cil qui plus fu enparlés des autres. "Dehait ore[1] qui por vous i cantera, biax sire!"

"Bel enfant," fait Aucassins, "enne me conissiés vos?"

"Oïl, nos savions bien que vos estes Aucassins nos damoisiax, mais nos ne somes mie a vos, ains somes au conte."

"Bel enfant, si ferés, je vos en pri."

"Os, por le cuerbé!" fait cil; "por quoi canteroie je por vos, s'il ne me seoit, quant il n'a si rice home en cest païs, sans le cors le conte Garin, s'il trovoit mé bués ne mes vaces ne mes brebis en ses prés n'en sen forment, qu'il fust mie tant herdis por les ex a crever qu'il les en ossast cacier? Et por quoi canteroie je por vos, s'il ne me seoit?"

"Se Dix vos aït, bel enfant, si ferés; et tenés dis sous que j'ai ci en une borse."

"Sire, les deniers prenderons nos, mais ce ne vos canterai mie, car j'en ai juré. Mais je le vos conterai, se vos volés."

"De par Diu," fait Aucassins, "encor aim je mix conter que nient."

"Sire, nos estiiens orains ci entre prime et tierce, si mangiens no pain a ceste fontaine, ausi con nos faisons ore; et une pucele vint ci, li plus bele riens du monde, si que nos quidames que ce fust une fee, et que tos cis bos en esclarci; si nos dona tant del[2] sien que nos li eumes en covent, se vos veniés ci, nos vos desisiens que vos alissiés cacier en ceste forest, qu'il i a une beste que, se vos le poiiés prendre, vos n'en donriiés mie un des menbres por cinc cens mars d'argent ne por nul avoir; car li beste a tel mecine que, se vos le poés prendre, vos serés garis de vo mehaig; et dedens trois jors le vos covien avoir prisse, et se vos ne l'avés prise, ja mais ne le verrés. Or le caciés se vos volés, et se vos volés si le laiscié, car je m'en sui bien acuités vers li."

"Bel enfant,"[3] fait Aucassins, "assés en avés dit, et Dix le me laist trover!"

50

Now they speak and tell and recount.
When Aucassin heard the shepherds, he thought of his sweet love Nicolette, whom he loved so much, and he realized that she had been there. And he spurred on his horse and rode right up to the shepherds.

"Pretty children, God save you!"

"God bless you!" said the one who was better-spoken than the others.

"Pretty children," said he, "repeat that song you were just singing."

"We won't repeat it," said he who was better-spoken than the others. "May God hate whoever sings it for you, dear sir."

"Pretty children," said Aucassin, "do you know who I am?"

"Yes, we know very well that you are our young lord Aucassin, but we are not your subjects; rather, we belong to the count."

"Pretty children, I beg you, please sing it."

"No, by God!" said he. "Why should I sing for you if it doesn't suit me, when there is no man in this country, except Count Garin himself, so rich that, if he found my oxen or cows or sheep in his fields or in his wheat, he would be brave enough to dare chase them away, at the risk of having his eyes put out? And why should I sing for you if it doesn't suit me?"

"God help you, pretty children, do it, and take ten sous that I have here in my purse."

"Sire, we'll take the coins, but we won't sing for you, because I've sworn not to. But I'll tell you the story, if you like."

"By God," said Aucassin, "I'd rather hear the story than nothing!"

"My lord, we were here, then, between prime and tierce, and we were eating our bread by this spring, as we were doing just now; and a maiden came along, the most beautiful creature in the world, so that we thought she was a fairy, and the whole forest lit up; and she gave us so much of what she had that we promised her that, if you came along, we would advise you that you should go hunting in this forest: there is such a beast here that, if you could catch it, you wouldn't sell even one of its limbs for five hundred silver marks, nor for any amount; for this beast has such power that, if you could catch it, you'd be cured of your illness; and you have to have caught it within three days, and if you haven't caught it, you'll never see it again. Now, go hunting for it if you like, or leave it alone if you prefer, because I have kept my word to her."

"Pretty children," said Aucassin, "you've said enough, and may God help me find it!"

23

Or se cante.

Aucassins oï les mos

de s'amie o le gent cors,

mout li entrerent el cors.

Des pastoriax se part tost,

si entra el parfont bos.

Li destriers li anble tost,

bien l'en porte les galos.

Or parla, s'a dit trois mos:

"Nicolete o le gent cors,

por vos sui venus en bos:

je ne cac ne cerf ne porc,

mais por vos siu les esclos.

Vo vair oiel et vos gens cors,

vos biax ris et vos dox mos

ont men cuer navré a mort.

Se Dix plaist le pere fort,

je vous reverai encor,

suer, douce amie!"

Now it is sung.

Our hero heard his fair one's words

and left the shepherds to their herds.

Her speech became a part of him.

He rode into the forest dim,

and gave the dashing horse his head,

and as he rode, these words he said:

"Noble-figured Nicolette,

I neither hunt a deer, nor yet

a boar—I search these woods for you:

I trace your path and heed your clue.

Your lovely laugh, your lively eyes,

your gentle words and noble guise

have given me a mortal sore:

I'm lovesick! But we'll meet once more—

if it pleases God so pure—

my sister, my sweet love."

24

O̶r dient et content et fabloient.

Aucassins ala par le forest de voie en voie et li destriers l'en porta grant aleure. Ne quidiés mie que les ronces et les espines l'esparnaiscent. Nenil nient! Ains li desronpent ses dras qu'a painnes peust on nouer desu el plus entier, et que li sans li isci des bras et des costés et des ganbes[1] en quarante lius u en trente, qu'après le vallet peust on suir le trace du sanc qui caoit sor l'erbe. Mais il pensa tant a Nicolete sa douce amie, qu'i ne sentoit ne mal ne dolor, et ala tote jor par mi le forest si faitement que onques n'oï noveles de li, et quant il vit que li vespres aproçoit, si comença a plorer por çou qu'il ne le trovoit.

Tote une viés voie herbeuse cevaucoit, s'esgarda devant lui en mi le voie, si vit un vallet tel con je vos dirai. Grans estoit et mervellex et lais et hidex. Il avoit une grande hure plus noire q'une carbouclee, et avoit plus de planne paume entre deus ex, et avoit unes grandes joes et un grandisme nes plat et unes grans narines lees et unes grosses levres plus rouges d'une carbounee et uns grans dens gaunes et lais; et estoit cauciés d'uns housiax et d'uns sollers de buef fretés de tille dusque deseure le genol, et estoit afulés d'une cape a deus envers, si estoit apoiiés sor une grande maçue.

Aucassins s'enbati sor lui, s'eut grant paor quant il le sorvit.

"Biax frere, Dix t'i aït!"

"Dix vos benie!" fait[2] cil.

"Se Dix t'aït, que fais tu ilec?"

"A vos que monte?" fait cil.

"Nient," fait Aucassins. "Je nel vos demant se por bien non."

"Mais por quoi plourés vos," fait cil, "et faites si fait duel? Certes, se j'estoie ausi rices hom que vos estes, tos li mons ne me feroit mie plorer."

"Ba! me connissiés vos?" fait Aucassins.

"Oie, je sai bien que vos estes Aucassins, li fix le conte, et se vos me dites por quoi vos plorés, je vos dirai que je fac ci."

"Certes," fait Aucassins, "je le vos dirai molt volentiers. Je vig hui matin cacier en ceste forest, s'avoie un blanc levrer, le plus bel del siecle, si l'ai perdu: por ce pleur jou."

"Os!" fait cil, "por le cuer que cil Sires eut en sen ventre! que vos plorastes por un cien puant? Mal dehait ait qui ja mais vos prisera, quant il n'a si rice home en ceste terre, se vos peres l'en mandoit dis u quinse u vint, qu'il ne les eust trop volentiers, et s'en esteroit trop liés. Mais je doi plorer et dol faire."

𝒩ow they speak and tell and recount.

Aucassin went through the forest from path to path, and his horse carried him swiftly. Don't imagine that the brambles and the thorns spared him. Not at all! On the contrary, they ripped up his clothes so that you could hardly have tied a knot in the least damaged bits, and the blood flowed out of his arms and his sides and his legs in forty places or thirty, so that someone coming after the young man could have followed the traces of his blood that fell on the grass. But he was so preoccupied by his sweet love Nicolette that he felt neither pain nor suffering, and all day long he continued through the forest just as ardently, without hearing any news of her, and when he saw that evening was approaching, he began to weep because he couldn't find her.

Riding along an old grassy pathway, he was looking at the path before him and saw a young man whom I am going to tell you about.[1] He was tall and looked bizarre, ugly and hideous. He had a big head, blacker than a lump of coal, and there was more than a hand's breadth between his two eyes, and he had a huge pair of cheeks and a gigantic flat nose and a pair of big, wide nostrils, and a thick pair of lips redder than a grilled steak, and a set of wide teeth, yellowed and ugly, and he was wearing leggings and a pair of shoes made of oxhide, laced up with linden bark above the knees, and he was wrapped up in a cape with two wrong sides, and he was leaning on a large mace.

Aucassin galloped up to him, and was terrified when he saw him up close.

"Fair friend, God save you!"

"God bless you," said the other.

"By God's protection, what are you doing here?"

"What's it to you?" said the other.

"Nothing," said Aucassin. "I meant no harm."

"But why are you weeping," said the other, "and making such sorrow? Surely, if I were as rich a man as you are, all the world together couldn't make me cry like that."

"Ah! Do you know me?" said Aucassin.

"Yes, I know perfectly well that you are Aucassin, the count's son, and if you tell me why you're crying, I'll tell you what I'm doing here."

"Certainly," said Aucassin, "I'll tell you most willingly. This morning I came here to this forest to hunt, and I had a white hound, the most beautiful one in the world, and I've lost it. That's why I'm weeping."

"No!" said the other, "by the Lord's heart in his chest, you're crying over some stinking dog? Bad luck to anyone who respects you, because no man in this land is so rich that if your father asked for ten or fifteen or twenty hounds, he wouldn't give them very willingly and be only too happy about it. But I'm the one who has a reason to weep and sorrow."

"Et tu de quoi, frere?"

"Sire, je le vous dirai. J'estoie luiés a un rice vilain, si caçoie se carue, quatre bués i avoit. Or a trois jors qu'il m'avint une grande malaventure, que je perdi le[3] mellor de mes bués, Roget, le mellor de me carue, si le vois querant, si ne mengai ne ne buc trois jors a passés, si n'os aler a le vile, c'on me metroit en prison, que je ne l'ai de quoi saure: de tot l'avoir du monde n'ai je plus vaillant que vos veés sor le cors de mi. Une lasse mere avoie, si n'avoit plus vaillant que une keutisele, si li a on sacie de desou le dos, si gist a pur l'estrain, si m'en poise assés plus que de mi; car avoirs va et vient: se j'ai or perdu, je gaaignerai une autre fois, si sorrai mon buef quant je porrai, ne ja por çou n'en plouerai. Et vos plorastes por un cien de longaigne? Mal dehait ait qui ja mais vos prisera!"

"Certes, tu es de bon confort, biax frere; que benois soies tu! Et que valoit tes bués?"

"Sire, vint sous m'en demande on; je n'en puis mie abatre une seule maaille."

"Or tien," fait Aucassins, "vint que j'ai ci en me borse, si sol ten buef."

"Sire," fait il, "grans mercis, et Dix vos laist trover ce que vos querés!"

Il se part de lui; Aucassins si cevauce. La nuis fu bele et quoie, et il erra tant qu'il vin[t pres de la u li set cemin aforkent] si v[it devant lui le loge que vos savés que] Nicolete [avoit faite, et le loge estoit forree][4] defors et dedens et par deseure et devant de flors, et estoit si bele que plus ne pooit estre. Quant Aucassins le perçut, si s'aresta tot a un fais, et li rais de le lune feroit ens.

"E Dix!" fait Aucassins, "ci fu Nicolete me douce amie, et ce fist ele a ses beles mains. Por le douçour de li et por s'amor me descenderai je ore ci et m'i reposerai anuit mais."

Il mist le pié fors de l'estrier por descendre, et li cevaus fu grans et haus; il pensa tant a Nicolete se tresdouce amie qu'il caï si durement sor une piere que l'espaulle li vola hors du liu. Il se senti molt blecié, mais il s'efforça tant au mix qu'il peut, et ataca son ceval a l'autre main a une espine, si se torna sor costé tant qu'il vint tos souvins en le loge. Et il garda par mi un trau de le loge, si vit les estoiles el ciel, s'en i vit une plus clere des autres, si conmença a dire:

"And for what reason, brother?"

"Sire, I'll tell you. I was working for a rich peasant[2] as his plowman, and I was looking after his team of four oxen. And three days ago a great misfortune befell me, for I lost the best of my oxen, Roget, the best of the team, and I went off looking for him, and I haven't eaten or drunk for the past three days, and I don't dare go back to town, because they'll put me in prison, since I have nothing to pay with: out of all the world's goods, I have nothing more valuable than what you see on my back. I had a poor mother, and she owned nothing more valuable than a mattress, and someone pulled it out from under her, so now she is lying on plain straw, and that weighs on me more than my own problems, for property comes and goes: if I have lost this time, another time I shall win, and I'll pay for the ox whenever I can, and I'd never cry over that. And you're crying over some shitty dog? To hell with anyone who respects you!"

"You're certainly a great comfort, fair brother; God bless you! And how much is your ox worth?"

"Sire, they're asking me for twenty sous:[3] I can't get them to come down even by a half penny."

"Now take," said Aucassin, "the twenty I have here in my purse, and pay for your ox."

"Sire," said he, "many thanks, and may God allow you to find what you're looking for."

He left him and Aucassin rode off. The night was beautiful and peaceful, and he rode on until he came to the place where the seven paths forked off, and saw before him the bower that you know Nicolette had built, and the bower was decorated inside and out, above and in front, with flowers, and was just as beautiful as it could be. When Aucassin noticed it, he stopped immediately, and a moonbeam fell onto it.

"Oh God!" said Aucassin, "it was my sweet love Nicolette who built this with her fair hands. Because of her sweetness and for love of her, I'll get down here and rest all night long."

He took his foot out of the stirrup in order to dismount, but his horse was big and high, and he was so preoccupied in thinking about his sweet love Nicolette that he fell onto a rock so heavily that his shoulder was dislocated. He felt himself to be seriously injured, but he forced himself as best he could, and, using his other hand, tied his horse to a thorn tree and turned over so that he could get into the bower on his back. And he looked through a chink in the bower, and saw the stars in the sky, and saw one that was brighter than the others, and began to say:

25

Or se cante.

"Estoilete, je te voi,

que la lune trait a soi.

Nicolete est aveuc toi,

m'amiëte o le blont poil.

Je quid Dix[1] le veut avoir[2]

por la lu[mier]e de s[oir]

[que par li plus bele soit.

Douce suer, com me plairoit

se monter pooie droit,][3]

que que fust du recaoir,

que fuisse lassus o toi!

Ja te baiseroie estroit.

Se j'estoie fix a roi,

s'afferriés vos bien a moi,

suer, douce amie."

*N*ow it is sung.

"I can see you, little star,[1]

the moon attracts you from afar.

Nicolette is with you there,

my lovely girl with golden hair.

I think God wants her there tonight

to beautify this evening light.

Sister sweet, how glad I'd be

if I could climb there too, so we

could be together! I would not

be scared of falling, if I got

up close enough to hold you tight;

I'd kiss you hard, with all my might.

Even were I royalty,

still you'd be just right for me,

my sister, my sweet love."

59

26

Or dient et content et fabloient.

Quant Nicolete oï Aucassin, ele vint a lui, car ele n'estoit mie lonc. Ele entra en la loge, si li jeta ses bras au col, si le baisa et acola.

"Biax doux amis, bien soiiés vos trovés!"

"Et vos, bele douce amie, soiés li bien trovee!"

Il s'entrebaissent et acolent, si fu la joie bele.

"Ha! douce amie," fait Aucassins, "j'estoie ore molt bleciés en m'espaulle, et or ne senc ne mal ne dolor, pui que je vos ai."

Ele le portasta et trova qu'il avoit l'espaulle hors du liu. Ele le mania tant a ses blances mains et porsaca, si con Dix le vaut qui les amans ainme, qu'ele revint a liu. Et puis si prist des flors et de l'erbe fresce et des fuelles verdes, si le loia sus au pan de sa cemisse, et il fu tox garis.

"Aucassins," fait ele, "biaus dox amis, prendés consel que vous ferés: se vos peres fait demain cerquier ceste forest et on me trouve, que que de vous aviegne, on m'ocira."

"Certes, bele douce amie, j'en esteroie molt dolans; mais, se je puis, il ne vos tenront ja."

Il monta sor son ceval et prent s'amie devant lui, baisant et acolant, si se metent as plains cans.

Now they speak and tell and recount.

When Nicolette heard Aucassin, she came to him, for she was not very far away. She entered the hut, and threw her arms around his neck, and kissed and hugged him.

"Fair sweet love, it's so good to find you!"

"And you, fair sweet love, it's so good to find you too!"

They kissed and hugged each other, and their joy was delightful.

"Ah! sweet love," said Aucassin, "just now my shoulder was badly injured, but now I feel neither pain nor suffering, because I have you."

She felt his shoulder all over and found that he had dislocated it. She handled it with her white hands and tugged at it so that, as God, who loves lovers, willed, it returned to its place. And then she took some flowers and fresh grass and green leaves, and tied them onto it with a piece of her skirt, and he was completely healed.

"Aucassin," said she, "fair sweet love, think about what you are going to do: if your father has this forest searched tomorrow and they find me, they'll kill me, whatever may become of you."

"Surely, fair sweet love, I'd be very grieved by that; but they won't take you if I can do anything about it."

He mounted his horse and took his love up in front of him; kissing and embracing, they made their way to the open plain.

27

Or se cante.[1]

Aucassins li biax, li blons,

li gentix, li amorous,

est issus del gaut parfont,

entre ses bras ses amors

devant lui sor son arçon;

les ex li baise et le front

et le bouce et le menton.

Ele l'a mis a raison:

"Aucassins, biax amis dox,

en quel tere en irons nous?"

"Douce amie, que sai jou?

Moi ne caut u nous aillons,

en forest u en destor,

mais que je soie aveuc vous."

Passent les vaus et les mons

et les viles et les bors;

a la mer vinrent au jor,

si descendent u sablon

les le rivage.

*N*ow it is sung.
Handsome, blond-haired Aucassin,
the noble, gentle, loving man,
issued from the forest dim;
between his arms, in front of him,
upon the saddle sat his love.
He kissed her forehead up above,
her eyes, her lips, and next her chin.
She questioned him, our heroine:
"Aucassin, my sweetest beau,
where do you intend to go?"
"How should I know, lover fair,
where we go? I do not care:
in forest or in Timbuktu,
as long as I can be with you."
Past vales and hills they took their way,
and cities, too. At break of day
they reached the seaside sands that lay
all along the shore.

28

Or dient et content et fabloient.

Aucassins fu descendus entre lui et s'amie, si con vous avés oï et entendu. Il tint son ceval par le resne et s'amie par le main, si conmencent aler selonc le rive. [Et Aucassins vit passer une nef, s'i aperçut les marceans qui sigloient tot prés de le rive.][1] Il les acena et il vinrent a lui, si fist tant vers aus qu'il les missent[2] en lor nef. Et quant il furent[3] en haute mer, une tormente leva, grande et mervelleuse, qui les mena de tere en tere, tant qu'il ariverent en une tere estragne et entrerent el port du castel de Torelore. Puis demanderent ques terre c'estoit, et on lor dist que c'estoit le tere le roi de Torelore; puis demanda quex hon c'estoit,[4] ne s'il avoit gerre, et on li dist:

"Oïl, grande."

Il prent congié as marceans et cil le conmanderent a Diu. Il monte sor son ceval, s'espee çainte, s'amie devant lui, et erra tant qu'il vint el castel. Il demande u li rois estoit, et on li dist qu'il gissoit d'enfent.

"Et u est dont se femme?"

Et on li dist qu'ele est en l'ost et si i avoit mené tox ciax du païs. Et Aucassins l'oï, si li vint a grant mervelle; et vint au palais et descendi entre lui et s'amie. Et ele tint son ceval et il monta u palais, l'espee çainte, et erra tant qu'il vint en[5] le canbre u li rois gissoit.

N̶ow they speak and tell and recount.

Aucassin had dismounted along with his love, as you have heard. He took his horse by the reins and his love by the hand, and they began to walk along the shore. [And Aucassin saw a ship passing, and noticed the merchants, who were sailing close to the shore.] He signaled them and they came in to him, and he persuaded them in such a way that they took them on board the ship. And when they were on the open sea, a great and marvelous storm blew up, which took them from country to country until they arrived in a strange land and entered the harbor of the castle of Torelore.[1] Then they asked what country it was, and they told them that it was the land of the king of Torelore. They asked what sort of man he was, and whether he was at war, and they told them:

"Yes, a great one."

He took his leave of the merchants, who commended him to God. He mounted his horse, his sword buckled on, his love in front of him, and rode until he came to the castle. He asked where the king was, and they told him that he was lying in childbed.

"And where is his wife, then?"

And they told him that she was with her army and was leading all the country's inhabitants.[2] And when Aucassin heard this, a great astonishment came over him; and he came to the palace and dismounted along with his love. And she held his horse and he climbed up the steps to the palace, his sword buckled on, and wandered around until he came into the chamber where the king was lying.

29

Or se cante.

En le canbre entre Aucassins,

li cortois et li gentis.

Il est venus dusque au lit,

alec u li rois se gist;

par devant lui s'arestit,

si parla; oés que dist:

"Di va! fau, que fais tu ci?"

Dist li rois: "Je gis d'un fil.

Quant mes mois sera conplis

et je sarai bien garis,

dont irai le messe oïr,

si com mes anc[estre fist,]¹

et me grant guerre esbaudir

encontre mes anemis:

nel lairai mie."

66

Now it is sung.

In the chamber Aucassin,

the courteous and noble man,

came right up before the bed

where the king had laid his head,

and stopped and spoke. Hear what he said:

"What are you doing, fool? Come on!"

The king said, "I've just had a son.[1]

Once I've done my lying-in,

I'll go be churched[2] like all my [kin;]

once I'm well I won't defer:

I'll then enjoy my battle, sir.

I won't neglect it."

30

Or dient et content et fabloient.[1]

Quant Aucassins oï ensi le roi parler, il prist tox les dras qui sor lui estoient, si les houla aval le canbre. Il vit deriere lui un baston, il le prist, si torne, si fiert, si le bati tant que mort le dut avoir.

"Ha! biax sire," fait li rois, "que me demandés vos? Avés vos le sens dervé, qui en me maison me batés?"

"Par le cuer Diu!" fait Aucassins, "malvais fix a putain, je vos ocirai, se vos ne m'afiés que ja mais hom en vo tere d'enfant ne gerra."

Il li afie; et quant il li ot afié:

"Sire," fait Aucassins, "or me menés la u vostre fenme est en l'ost."

"Sire, volentiers," fait li rois.

Il monte sor un ceval, et Aucassins monte sor le sien, et Nicolete remest es canbres la roine. Et li rais et Aucassins cevaucierent tant qu'il vinrent la u la roine estoit, et troverent la bataille de poms de bos waumonnés et d'ueus et de fres fromages. Et Aucassins les conmença a regarder, se s'en esmevella molt durement.

ℐow they speak and tell and recount.

When Aucassin heard the king speaking in this way, he took all the bedclothes that were covering him and threw them to the other end of the room. He noticed a staff behind him, took it, and turned around and struck him, and beat him until he thought he'd die.

"Ah, dear sir!" said the king, "what do you want of me? Are you deranged, to beat me in my own house?"

"By God's heart!" said Aucassin, "evil son of a whore, I'll kill you, unless you promise me that no man in your country will ever lie in childbed again."

He promised him; and when he had sworn,

"Sire," said Aucassin, "now take me there where your wife is with the army."

"Certainly, sir," said the king.

He mounted a horse, and Aucassin mounted his own, and Nicolette remained in the queen's chamber. And the king and Aucassin rode until they came to where the queen was, and found the battle being conducted with rotten apples and with eggs and with fresh cheeses.[1] And Aucassin began watching them, and was greatly astonished.

31

Or se cante.[1]

Aucassins est arestés,

sor son arçon acoutés,

si coumence a regarder

ce plenier estor canpel.

Il avoient aportés

des fromages fres assés

et puns de bos waumonés

et grans canpegneus canpés.

Cil qui mix torble les gués

est li plus sire clamés.

Aucassins, li prex, li ber,

les coumence a regarder,

s'en prist a rire.

Now it is sung.

On his saddle, Aucassin

halted, and began to scan

the place where this great war was fought.

The soldiers on both sides had brought

fresh cheeses, rotten apples, and

big mushrooms gathered in that land.

Whoever best disturbed the ford

was there proclaimed the noblest lord.

The noble, valiant Aucassin

had to laugh when he began

to watch this fight.

32

Or dient et content et flabent.

Quant Aucassins vit cele mervelle, si vint au roi, si l'apele.

"Sire," fait Aucassins, "sont ce ci vostre anemi?"

"Oïl, sire," fait li rois.

"Et vouriiés vos que je vos en venjasse?"

"Oie," fait il, "volentiers."

Et Aucassins met le main a l'espee, si se lance en mi ax, si conmence a ferir a destre et a senestre, et s'en ocit molt. Et quant li rois vit qu'i les ocioit, il le prent par le frain et dist:

"Ha! biax sire, ne les ociés mie si faitement."

"Conment?" fait Aucassins. "En volés vos que je vos venge?"

"Sire," dist li rois, "trop en avés vos fait: il n'est mie costume que nos entrocions li uns l'autre."

Cil tornent en fuies; et li rois et Aucassins s'en repairent au castel de Torelore. Et les gens del païs dient au roi qu'il cast Aucassins fors de sa tere, et si detiegne Nicolete aveuc son fil, qu'ele sanbloit bien fenme de haut lignage. Et Nicolete l'oï, si n'en fu mie lie, si conmença a dire.

$\mathcal{N}$*ow they speak and tell and recount.*
When Aucassin saw this marvel, he came to the king and spoke to him.

"Sire," said Aucassin, "are those your enemies?"

"Yes, sir," said the king.

"And would you like me to avenge you on them?"

"Yes," said he, "gladly."

And Aucassin put his hand to his sword, and launched himself into their midst, and began striking blows on the right and on the left, and he killed many of them. And when the king saw that he was killing them, he took hold of the bridle and said:

"Ah, dear sir, don't kill them like that!"

"What?" said Aucassin. "Don't you want me to avenge you?"

"Sir," said the king, "you've gone too far: it isn't our custom to kill one another."

The others turned and fled, and the king and Aucassin returned to the castle of Torelore. And the people of the region told the king to throw Aucassin out of the country, and to keep Nicolette there with his son, for she appeared to be a woman of high lineage. And Nicolette heard this clearly, and was not a bit pleased with it, and began to speak:

73

33

Or se cante.

"Sire rois de Torelore,"

ce dist la bele Nichole,

"vostre gens me tient por fole:

quant mes dox amis m'acole

et il me sent grasse et mole,

dont sui jou a tele escole,

baus ne tresce ne carole,

harpe, gigle ne viole,

ne deduis de la nimpole

n'i vauroit mie."

74

Now it is sung.

"Sir king of Torelore," she said,

"you all may think I'm off my head,

but when my love embraces me,

and feels my softness, tenderly,

within I feel such blossomings,

no song or dance, or other things,

or viol, harp, or violin,

or ladies' games,[1] though I should win,

are worth a thing to me."

34

Or dient et content et flaboient.

Aucassins fu el castel de Torelore, et Nicolete s'amie, a grant aise et a grant deduit, car il avoit aveuc lui Nicolete sa douce amie que tant amoit.

En ço qu'il estoit en tel aisse et en tel deduit, et uns estores de Sarrasins vinrent par mer, s'asalirent au castel, si le prissent par force. Il prissent l'avoir, s'en menerent caitis et kaítives; il prissent Nicolete et Aucassin, et si loierent Aucassin les mains et les piés, et si le jeterent en une nef et Nicolete[1] en une autre; si leva une tormente par mer que les espartist.

Li nés u Aucassins estoit ala tant par mer waucrant qu'ele ariva au castel de Biaucaire; et les gens du païs cururent au lagan, si troverent Aucassin, si le reconurent. Quant cil de Biaucaire virent lor damoisel, s'en fisent grant joie, car Aucassins avoit bien mes u castel de Torelore trois ans, et ses peres et se mere estoient mort. Il le menerent u castel de Biaucaire, si devinrent tot si home, si tint se tere en pais.

Now they speak and tell and recount.

Aucassin was living in the castle of Torelore, with his love Nicolette, in great pleasure and great delight, because he had his sweet love Nicolette with him, whom he loved so much.

While he was living in such pleasure and such delight, a fleet of Saracens arrived by sea; they assaulted the castle and took it by force.[1] They seized their goods and took the men and women prisoner; they took Nicolette and Aucassin, and bound Aucassin hand and foot, and threw him in one ship and Nicolette in another; and a tempest arose at sea, which separated them.

The ship in which Aucassin was, was driven over the sea until it arrived at the castle of Beaucaire; and the people of that land ran to pillage it, and found Aucassin, and recognized him. When the people of Beaucaire saw their young lord, they made great joy, for Aucassin had been in the castle of Torelore for three years, and his father and mother were dead. They led him to the castle of Beaucaire, and became his vassals, and he held his land in peace.

35

Or se cante.

Aucassins s'en est alés

a Biaucaire sa cité.

Le païs et le regné

tint trestout en quiteé.

Jure Diu de maïsté

qu'il[1] li poise plus assés

de Nicholete au vis cler

que de tot sen parenté

s'il estoit a fin alés.

"Douce amie o le vis cler,

or ne vous ai u quester;

ainc Diu ne fist ce regné

ne par terre ne par mer,

se t'i quidoie trover,

ne t'i quesisce."

Now it is sung.

Aucassin once more has found

Beaucaire. And now the realm around,

his land and folk, he ruled in peace,

without a threat. He does not cease

to swear to God in majesty

that deeper in distress is he

for Nicolette, so fair to see,

than his extinguished family.[1]

"My fair, sweet love, I have no clue;

I don't know where to look for you,

though God has made no country where,

if I thought I'd find you there,

I would be afraid to dare

search for you."

36

Or dient et content et fabloien.

Or lairons d'Aucassin, si dirons de Nicolete.

La nes u Nicolete estoit estoit[1] le roi de Cartage, et cil estoit ses peres, et si avoit dose freres, tox princes u rois. Quant il virent Nicolete si bele, se li porterent molt grant honor et fisent feste de li, et molt li demanderent qui ele estoit, car molt sanbloit bien gentix fenme et de haut. Mais ele ne lor sot a dire qui ele estoit, car ele fu pree petis enfes. Il nagierent tant qu'il ariverent desox le cité de Cartage, et quant Nicolete vit les murs del castel et le païs, ele se reconut, qu'ele i avoit esté norie et pree petis enfes, mais ele ne fu mie si petis enfes que ne seust bien qu'ele avoit esté fille au roi de Cartage et qu'ele avoit esté norie en le cité.

80

Now they speak and tell and recount.

Now let us leave Aucassin and speak of Nicolette.

The ship where Nicolette was, was that of the king of Carthage, and he was her father, and she had twelve brothers, all princes or kings. When they saw Nicolette was so beautiful, they greatly honored her and made great joy over her, and repeatedly asked who she was, for she very much seemed to be a real, high-born gentlewoman. But she didn't know what to tell them about who she was, for she had been captured as a small child. They sailed until they arrived before the city of Carthage, and when Nicolette saw the castle walls and the countryside, she knew who she was, that she had been raised here and captured as a small child, but she had not been so small a child that she didn't know perfectly well that she was the daughter of the king of Carthage and that she had been raised in this city.

37

Or se cante.

Nichole li preus, li sage,

est arivee a rivage,

voit les murs et les astages

et les palais et les sales;

dont si s'est clamee lasse:

"Tant mar fui de haut parage,

ne fille au roi de Cartage,

ne cousine l'amuaffle!

Ci me mainnent gent sauvage.

Aucassin gentix et sages,

frans damoisiax honorables,

vos douces amors me hastent

et semonent et travaillent.

Ce doinst Dix l'esperitables

c'oncor vous tiengne en me brace,

et que vos baissiés me face

et me bouce et mon visage,

damoisiax sire."

Now it is sung.

The clever, wise, and brave Nicole

has reached the coast, her captors' goal.

She sees the houses and the walls,

and all the palaces and halls,

for which she feels she must lament:

"Alas that I'm of high descent,

a pagan princess, also near

relation to the Grand Emir![1]

I'm brought here by my savage clan.

Oh wise and noble Aucassin,

my lord, so honest, young, and free,

your love is sweet; it hurries me,

and draws me on, a welcome prod.

I pray the heavenly spirit, God,

that we two may again embrace,

that I may see you, by his grace,

so you can kiss my lips and face,

my young lord."

38

Or dient et content et fabloient.

Quant li rois de Cartage oï Nicolete ensi parler, il li geta ses bras au col.

"Bele douce amie," fait il, "dites moi qui vos estes. Ne vos esmaiiés mie de mi."

"Sire," fait ele, "je sui fille au roi de Cartage et fui preée petis enfes, bien a quinse ans."

Quant il l'oïrent ensi parler, si seurent bien qu'ele disoit voir, si fissen de li molt grant feste, si le menerent u palais a grant honeur, si conme fille de roi. Baron li vourent doner un roi de paiiens, mais ele n'avoit cure de marier. La fu bien trois jors u quatre. Ele se porpensa par quel engien ele porroit Aucassin querre. Ele quist une viele, s'aprist a vieler, tant c'on le vaut marier un jor a un roi rice paiien. Et ele s'enbla la nuit, si vint au port de mer, si se herbega ciés une povre fenme sor le rivage. Si prist une herbe, si en oinst son cief et son visage, si qu'ele fu tote noire et tainte. Et ele fist faire cote et mantel et cemisse et braies, si s'atorna a guise de jogleor, si prist se viele, si vint a un marounier, se fist tant vers lui qu'il le mist en se nef. Il drecierent lor voile, si nagierent tant par haute mer qu'il ariverent en le terre de Provence. Et Nicolete issi fors, si prist se viele, si ala vielant par le païs tant qu'ele vint au castel de Biaucaire, la u Aucassins estoit.

N̶ow they speak and tell and recount.

When the king of Carthage heard Nicolette speaking in this way, he threw his arms around her neck.

"Beautiful sweet love," said he, "tell me who you are! You have nothing to fear from me."

"My lord," said she, "I am the daughter of the king of Carthage, and was captured as a small child, some fifteen years ago."

When they heard her speaking in this manner, they knew she was telling the truth, and took great joy in her, and brought her to the palace in great honor, as befitted a king's daughter. They wanted to give her a pagan king for a husband, but she had no wish to be married. She spent three or four days there. She thought about the means by which she might seek Aucassin. She acquired a viol and learned how to play it, until one day they wanted to marry her to a rich pagan king. And that night she fled, and came to the seaport, and took refuge with a poor woman living on the shore. She took an herb and anointed her head and face with it, so that she was stained completely black. And she had a tunic and a cloak and a shirt and breeches made, and took on the appearance of a minstrel,[1] and took up her viol, and approached a mariner, and talked him into letting her on board. They raised the sails and navigated the high seas until they reached the land of Provence. And Nicolette left the ship with her viol, and traveled through the country playing it until she came to the castle of Beaucaire, where Aucassin was.

39

Or se cante.[1]

A Biaucaire sous la tor

estoit Aucassins un jor,

la se sist sor un perron,

entor lui si franc baron.

Voit les herbes et les flors

s'oit canter les oisellons,

menbre li de ses amors,

de Nicholete le prox

qu'il ot amee tans jors;

dont jete souspirs et plors.

Es vous Nichole au peron,

trait vïele, trait arçon.

Or parla, dist sa raison:

"Escoutés moi, franc baron

cil d'aval et cil d'amont:

plairoit vos oïr un son

d'Aucassin, un franc baron,

de Nicholete la prous?

Tant durerent lor amors

qu'il le quist u gaut parfont.

A Torelore u dongon

les prissent paiien un jor.

D'Aucassin rien ne savons,

Now it is sung.

Upon a bench of stone one day,

beneath the keep, our hero lay,

surrounded by his barons free.

Grass and flowers he could see,

and hearing all the birds' sweet song,

he thought of love, which made him long

for Nicolette, so brave and gay,

whom he had loved for many a day;

he sighed for her, and wept. But see!

Nicole was at his side, and she

took up her viol and her bow,

and then she told about her show:

"Hear me now, my barons free,

those of low and high degree:

will you hear about a man,

a baron free, lord Aucassin,

and the valiant Nicolette?

Their hearts were on each other set

so firmly that he hunted for

her through the woods. At Torelore,

in the castle there one day,

pagans seized them. Who can say

what became of Aucassin?

mais Nicolete la prous

est a Cartage el donjon,

car ses pere l'ainme mout

qui sire est de cel roion.

Doner li volent baron

un roi de paiiens felon.

Nicolete n'en a soing,

car ele aime un dansellon

qui Aucassins avoit non;

bien jure Diu et son non,[2]

ja ne prendera baron,

s'ele n'a son ameor

que tant desire."

But her father's pagan clan
has captured brave Nicole. Although
she doesn't want to, she must go
to Carthage, where her father's king
and loves her more than anything.
And now they want to make her wed
a felon pagan king," she said.
"She won't, because another man
has won her heart: young Aucassin.
She swears to God upon his name
no other man will ever claim
her as his wife, except her flame,
the love she so desires."

O̶r dient et content et fabloient.

Quant Aucassins oï ensi parler Nicolete, il fu molt liés, si le traist d'une part, se li demanda:

"Biax dous amis," fait Aucassins, "savés vos nient de cele Nicolete dont vos avés ci canté?"

"Sire, oie, j'en sai con de le plus france creature et de le plus gentil et de le plus sage qui onques fust nee; si est fille au roi de Cartage, qui le prist la u Aucassins fu pris, si le mena en le cité de Cartage tant qu'il seut bien[1] que c'estoit se fille, si en fist molt grant feste. Si li veut on doner cascun jor baron un des plus haus rois de tote Espaigne; mais ele se lairoit ançois pendre u ardoir qu'ele en presist nul, tant fust rices."

"Ha! Biax dox amis," fait li quens Aucassins, "se vous voliiés raler en cele terre, se li dississçiés qu'ele venist a mi parler, je vos donroie de mon avoir tant con vos en oseriés demander ne prendre. Et saciés que por l'amor de li ne voul je prendre fenme, tant soit de haut parage, ains l'atenc, ne ja n'arai fenme se li non. Et se je le seusce u trover, je ne l'eusce ore mie a querre."

"Sire," fait ele, "se vos çou faissiés, je l'iroie querre por vos et por li que je molt aim."

Il li afie, et puis se li fait doner vint livres. Ele se part de lui, et il pleure por le douçor de Nicolete; et quant ele le voit plorer:

"Sire," fait ele, "ne vos esmaiiés pas, que dusqu'a pou le vos arai en ceste vile amenee, se que vos le verrés."

Et quant Aucassins l'oï, si en fu molt liés. Et ele se part de lui, si traist en le vile a le maison le viscontesse, car li visquens ses parrins estoit mors. Ele se herbega[2] la, si parla a li tant qu'ele li gehi son afaire et que le viscontesse le recounut et seut bien que c'estoit Nicolete et qu'ele l'avoit norrie. Si le fist laver et baignier et sejorner uit jors tous plains.

Si prist une herbe qui avoit non esclaire, si s'en oinst, si fu ausi bele qu'ele avoit onques esté a nul jor. Se se vesti de rices dras de soie, dont la dame avoit assés, si s'assist en le canbre sor une cueute pointe de drap de soie, si apela la dame et li dist qu'ele alast por Aucassin son ami. Et ele si fist, et quant ele vint u palais, si trova Aucassin qui ploroit et regretoit Nicolete s'amie, por çou qu'ele demouroit tant; et la dame l'apela, si li dist:

"Aucassins, or ne vos dementés plus, mais venés ent aveuques mi et je vos mosterai la riens el mont que vos amés plus, car c'est Nicolete vo duce amie, qui de longes terres vos est venue querre."

Et Aucassins fu liés.

Now they speak and tell and recount.
When Aucassin heard Nicolette speaking in this way, he was overjoyed, and took her to one side, and asked her:

"Fair sweet friend," said Aucassin, "do you know anything about this Nicolette of whom you have been singing?"

"Yes, my lord, I know of her as the most generous creature, and the noblest and wisest who ever was born; and she is the daughter of the king of Carthage, who captured her there where Aucassin was taken, and brought her to the city of Carthage, so that he realized she was his daughter, and he greatly rejoiced over her. And every day he wanted to give her one of the highest kings in all of Spain for her husband; but she would rather be hanged or burned than accept any of them, no matter how rich."

"Ah! Fair, sweet friend," said Count Aucassin, "if you would like to return to that land and tell her that she should come and speak to me, I will give you as much of my wealth as you could dare ask or accept. And let me tell you that for love of her I don't wish to take a wife, no matter how noble her lineage; instead, I am waiting for her, and will have no other wife but her. And if I had known where to find her, I wouldn't have to look for her now."

"My lord," said she, "if you would do that, I'd go look for her, for you and for her whom I love so much."

He promised, and then had her given twenty pounds. She took her leave, and he wept over the sweetness of Nicolette; and when she saw him weeping:

"My lord," said she, "don't be dismayed, for before long I shall have brought her to you in this city, as you shall see."

And when Aucassin heard her, he was overjoyed. And she left him, and went to the viscountess's house in the city, for her godfather, the viscount, was dead. She lodged there, and talked with her until she had revealed her whole story, and the viscountess recognized her and realized that it was Nicolette and that she had raised her. She had her washed and bathed, and she stayed there a full eight days.

She took an herb called celandine and anointed herself, and she was just as beautiful as she had been at any time. She dressed herself in rich robes of silk, of which the lady had plenty, and sat down in her chamber on a coverlet of silk, and called the lady and told her that she should go for Aucassin, her love. And the lady did, and when she came to the palace, she found Aucassin, who was crying and longing for his love Nicolette, because she was so long in coming; and the lady called out to him, and said to him:

"Aucassin, don't distress yourself any longer, but come along with me and I'll show you the creature you love most in the world, for it is your sweet love Nicolette, who has come looking for you from far-off lands."

And Aucassin was happy.

41

Or se cante.

Quant or entent Aucassins

de s'amie o le cler vis

qu'ele est venue el païs,

or fu liés, ainc ne fu si.

Aveuc la dame s'est mis,

dusqu'a l'ostel ne prist fin.

En le cambre se sont mis,

la u Nicholete sist.

Quant ele voit son ami,

or fu lie, ainc ne fu si.

Contre lui en piés sali.

Quant or le voit Aucassins,

andex ses bras li tendi,

doucement le recoulli,

les eus li baisse et le vis.

La nuit le laissent ensi,

tresqu'au demain par matin

que l'espousa Aucassins:

dame de Biaucaire en fist.

Puis vesquirent il mains dis

Et menerent lor delis.

Or a sa joie Aucasins

et Nicholete autresi:

no cantefable prent fin,

n'en sai plus dire.

Now it is sung.

Now when Aucassin has heard,

about his shining love, the word

that she's back on his native shore,

then he was joyful, never more.

The lady brings him back with her

directly to the wanderer,

to Nicolette on her divan.

When she saw her darling man,

she was filled with joy and bliss

and ran to greet him with a kiss.

When he saw that it was she,

he embraced her tenderly,

kissed her on the eyes and face.

That night they shared just one embrace.

But in the morning Aucassin

married her; that noble man

made her the lady of Beaucaire.

They lived long lives without a care.

Now Aucassin and Nicolette

have found their joy, and I intend

to grant our story-song its end,

for I've no more to say.

Notes to the Old French Text

1

1. "Qui" can be understood as a relative pronoun, but I follow several other editors in reading it as an interrogative, and therefore in placing a question mark at the end of line 7.
2. biax li dis] biax est li dis. The manuscript reading brings the number of syllables in the line to eight, whereas the music and consistency with most other lines in the verse passages require seven. Similar adjustments have been made elsewhere.

2

1. The manuscript's spelling "rai" is unusual, but not unique in the Picard dialect. I follow Anne Elizabeth Cobby's edition in retaining the manuscript spelling rather than normalizing it to "roi" as some editors have done: see her note on this line in *Aucassin and Nicolette*, in *The Pilgrimage of Charlemagne (Le Pèlerinage de Charlemagne); Aucassin and Nicolette (Aucassin et Nicolette)*, ed. and trans. Glyn S. Burgess and Anne Elizabeth Cobby (New York: Garland, 1988).

3

1. This line could equally well be assigned to Aucassin or to his mother.
2. The manuscript has "prem femme" at this point (the beginning of a new gathering), but the catchwords at the bottom of the preceding column are "pren femme."
3. mesclaire] melcraire

4

1. avoir] et avoir
2. The manuscript reading is unclear; it could be either "Ce" or "Or."

5

1. The manuscript gives no music for the second line.
2. n'i] l ni

6

1. Nicolete] Aic'.
2. en] e
3. croutes] cuutes

4. buen] bien
5. se se] ise se

8
1. li] le

9
1. sissent es] sissent. The extra syllable is added for metrical reasons.
2. le] li

10
1. The initial A is obscured in the manuscript.
2. il le] i l
3. feroient] foroient
4. a ferir a] a
5. ans] a
6. j'aroie] lairoi ie
7. ce voil je que] je voil je
8. je] ce
9. fait] fiat

11
1. m'i] ni

12
1. del] des
2. ses] sans

15
1. un cant] uns cans

16
1. del] des
2. ele] il

17
1. il i a a] il i a. The extra syllable is added for metrical reasons.
2. mix assés] nix asses

18
1. Entreusque il] entreusqui il

2. enfant, fait ele] enfait ele
3. fait ele] fait
4. qu'il a] quela

19
1. cemin] cenin
2. ne] ne ne

20
1. vient] vent

21
1. au corset] au cors corset

22
1. Dehait ore] dehait a ore
2. del] des
3. enfant] enfait

24
1. ganbes] gans
2. fait] fiat
3. le] li
4. The manuscript is torn at this point; Hermann Suchier first supplied the conjectural readings here marked off by brackets in his edition, *Aucassin und Nicolette*, 8th ed. (Paderborn, Germany: Ferdinand Schöning, 1913), and they have been widely accepted.

97

25
1. Dix] que Dix. A syllable is omitted for metrical reasons.
2. This word is now partially obscured by a repair to the manuscript, but it is visible in Bourdillon's facsimile edition.
3. Once again, like other editors, I adopt Suchier's conjectures for the lines missing due to the tear in the manuscript, and mark them off by brackets.

27
1. cante] can

28
1. A transitional sentence appears to have been omitted from the manuscript here. Again, Suchier's conjecture appears in brackets.

2. qu'il les missent] This brief passage has been obscured in the manuscript by scraping. I adopt Suchier's reading.
3. The initial f of "furent" is obscured in the manuscript by the scraping described in note 2.
4. c'estoit] c'est ot ["ot" written in above the line]
5. en] e

29
1. This line is incomplete due to a tear in the manuscript; Gaston Paris supplied the missing words in his edition, *Aucassin et Nicolette, chantefable du XIIe siècle*, ed. Gaston Paris, trans. Alexandre Bida (Paris: Hachette, 1878), and his suggestions are widely accepted.

30
1. fabloient] faboient

31
1. cante] cant

34
1. Nicolete] Aucassin

35
1. qu'il] qui il

36
1. estoit estoit] estoit

39
1. The word "cante" is now mostly obscured by the manuscript binding. It is also invisible in Bourdillon's facsimile, but he includes it in his transcription.
2. son non] son

40
1. seut bien] seut bm
2. herbega] h'ga

Explanatory Notes to the English Translation

1

1. This line has caused much scholarly disagreement. Some earlier editors emended it in various ways, but more recent ones retain the manuscript reading, as I do here. The term "viel antif" is both redundant and ambiguous, but the same ambiguity occurs in section 19, and need not pose a problem. I understand the term as a reference to the author.
2. The term "biax enfans petis" literally means "beautiful little children," but the lovers are clearly not to be understood as children in the modern sense. Section 37 indicates that Nicolette is more than fifteen years old, while Aucassin is old enough to be expected to fight in the battles against Bougars de Valence.
3. Ironically, Nicolette, the Saracen, is named for a Christian saint, while Aucassin's name appears to be Arabic: Dufournet in his edition, *Aucassin et Nicolette: édition critique*, 2nd ed. (Paris: Garnier-Flammarion, 1984), relates it to Alcazin, the king of Cordova from 1019–1021 as well as to the Provençal diminutive *aucassa*, "goose."
4. The feminine "douce" could refer either to an unexpressed term for "tale," e.g., "cante fable," or to Nicolette, who is also given healing powers later in the text. I understand "douce" as a reference to the tale itself, hence "it" rather than "she."

2

1. The formula "Or dient et content et fablent," which, with some variations, introduces the following prose section at the end of each verse section, indicates speech and narration rather than song; the terms are somewhat redundant, but critical attempts to give them any greater significance have not proven convincing.
2. The name "Bougars" suggests "bogre" or "bougeron," terms associated with both heresy and sodomy; if "Valence" refers to Valencia in Spain, an association with Islam is also implied because of Spain's occupation by Muslims ("Saracens" in the text's terminology). The count thus becomes a sign of various anxieties threatening Christian Europe, at least in its own cultural imagination.
3. The only siege in which the Provençal city of Beaucaire was involved in the thirteenth century took place in the course of the Albigensian Crusade, under conditions similar to those described here, as Robert Griffin points out in "*Aucassin et Nicolette* and the Albigensian Crusade," *Modern Language Quarterly* 26 (1965): 243–56.

4. The French term "sergens" is clearly contrasted with "cevaliers" or knights, and indicates a soldier of non-aristocratic status; Eugene Vance, "*Aucassin et Nicolette* and the Poetics of Discourse," in his *Marvelous Signals: Poetics and Sign Theory in the Middle Ages* (Lincoln: University of Nebraska Press, 1986), 152–83, at 159, argues convincingly that they are in fact to be understood as mercenaries.
5. The French text uses both the terms "vallet" and "damoisiax" to describe Aucassin, terms that overlap in meaning: both are used to refer to a young man of noble birth who had not yet become a knight. "Vallet" emphasizes youth, and is close in meaning to the English "squire": a "vallet" would assist a knight in arming and disarming, carry messages for him, etc. "Damoisiax" emphasizes nobility, and might also be applied to a young knight, a status to which Aucassin has not yet acceded, but which seems imminent. I translate the terms as "young gentleman" and "young nobleman."
6. The French term is "baceler," another term overlapping in meaning with "vallet." Typically the "baceler" is an unmarried young nobleman or knight in the service of a lord. Apparently Count Garin sees his own son as occupying a higher social status.

3

1. Line 5 is difficult to interpret; other translators render it differently.
2. The French text refers to "Cartage," which is usually taken to mean the Islamic Spanish city of Cartagena, but Cobby in her edition points out that it could equally well refer to Carthage. Either city fits the sense of the text, which requires only that Nicolette be a native of some wealthy and powerful Islamic city.
3. "Saisne" typically means "Saxon," as in Jean Bodel's *Chanson des Saisnes*, not "Saracen"; here it may be used as a generic term for "pagan."

5

1. Nicolette must later climb down from this room in order to escape; in reality, however, rooms above the ground floor would not have been vaulted, as Dufournet points out in his edition's note on this line.

6

1. Few critics have taken Aucassin's ensuing diatribe seriously, but it is clearly heretical, and may be understood in the context of the various types of resistance to normative behavior found throughout the text.
2. The French term "baron" can refer either to a nobleman, as in section 39, or to a husband, as here.
3. The French terms "vair" and "gris" refer to prized furs from different parts of the gray squirrel: "vair" is the white fur of the underside, "gris" the gray fur of the back.

4. A "jogleor" or *jongleur* might provide various kinds of entertainment, including poetry, music, and storytelling as well as acrobatics, fire-eating, etc. Nicolette disguises herself as such a minstrel in sections 38–40.

9
1. A cuirass made with double rows of chain mail.
2. A shield with a metal boss.

10
1. A riding horse as distinct from a warhorse or "destrier."

18
1. The French term "haute prime" suggests that the hour of prime is well past, but that the hour of tierce has not yet arrived. Prime and tierce are both examples of the monastic time-keeping scheme (geared to the hours at which different liturgies were sung) commonly found in medieval literature, a less exact scheme than modern clock time. "Prime" corresponds more or less to 6:00 a.m., "tierce" more or less to 9:00 a.m., though there were wide local fluctuations. Nicolette thus sleeps until around 7:30.
2. Fairies are powerful and often frightening beings in medieval folklore.

20
1. "None" is another example of monastic time, corresponding roughly to 3:00 p.m. See section 18, note 1.

21
1. See section 24, note 3, on monetary values.

24
1. The following description draws on the traditional attributes of giants, but also on the ugliness traditionally attributed to peasants, and thus represents an intersection of class and racial—or even species—differences.
2. The French term "vilain" carries pejorative connotations, not unlike the English term "peasant" in some current usages.
3. In medieval French monetary transactions, a "maille" is worth half a "denier"; there are twelve "deniers" in a "sou" and twenty "sous" in a "livre."

25
1. Presumably the planet Venus, often associated with both love and the moon.

28

1. The name "Torelore" is derived from the nonsense refrains of popular songs; an equivalent in English would be "Tooraloora."
2. These details mark Torelore as a site of carnivalesque gender inversion. It is unclear whether we are to regard the king as engaged in the folk ritual of couvade (the male imitation of female lying-in) or as actually having given birth; if the latter, the inhabitants of Torelore are also a comical version of the monstrous races imagined as living beyond the borders of Europe in many medieval texts, and thus perhaps as a comical displacement of the "monstrous" Saracens.

29

1. This line continues the ambiguity noted in section 28, note 2.
2. The ceremony in which a woman normally returned to church for the first time after a confinement and gave thanks for the newborn child (and her own survival).

30

1. This detail marks Torelore as a site of further inversions beyond those of gender: the harmlessness of this warfare incites Aucassin to engage in precisely the normative chivalric behavior that he eschews in his native land, and to attempt to impose this European-style behavior on Torelore, whose inhabitants reject it in section 32.

33

1. "Nimpole," according to Mario Roques's glossary, may refer to some sort of board game.

34

1. "Saracen" is a name regularly applied to Muslims in Western European medieval literature, though they are typically represented as pagans, as they are here, rather than as monotheistic practitioners of Islam. Western Europe's obsession with Islam and the threat it supposedly posed to Christendom appears throughout medieval literature, especially during the period of the Crusades.

35

1. Some critics have found it odd that Aucassin does not actually search for Nicolette at this point, but this is only one example of Aucassin's passivity, to be contrasted with the more active character of Nicolette, especially in the following sections.

37

1. The Old French term "amuaffle" is one of many terms conventionally signifying a Saracen leader.

38

1. Nicolette here crosses both gender and class boundaries, and perhaps ethnic and religious ones as well, though the darkened face might be taken primarily as a sign of lower-class status, as in the earlier description of the peasant cowherd.

Bibliography

For additional resources, see also Sargent-Baur, Barbara Nelson, and Robert Francis Cook. *Aucassin et Nicolette: A Critical Bibliography*. London: Grant and Cutler, 1981.

Facsimile

Bourdillon, F. W., ed. *Cest dAucasī & de Nicolete*. Oxford: Clarendon, 1896.

Major Editions

Bourdillon, F. W., ed. *Aucassin et Nicolette*. 3rd ed. 1919; repr. Manchester: University of Manchester Press, 1930.

Dufournet, Jean, ed. and trans. *Aucassin et Nicolette: édition critique*. 2nd ed. Paris: Garnier-Flammarion, 1984.

Paris, Gaston, ed., and Alexandre Bida, trans. *Aucassin et Nicolette, chantefable du XIIIe siècle*. Paris: Hachette, 1878.

Roques, Mario, ed. *Aucassin et Nicolette: Chantefable du XIIIe siècle*. 2nd ed. Paris: Champion, 1963.

Suchier, Hermann, ed. *Aucassin und Nicolette*. 8th ed. Paderborn, Germany: Ferdinand Schöning, 1913.

Modern English Translations

Cobby, Anne Elizabeth, ed. and trans. *Aucassin and Nicolette*. In *The Pilgrimage of Charlemagne (Le Pèlerinage de Charlemagne); Aucassin and Nicolette (Aucassin et Nicolette)*, ed. and trans. Glyn S. Burgess and Anne Elizabeth Cobby. New York: Garland, 1988.

Matarasso, Pauline, trans. *Aucassin and Nicolette and Other Tales*. Harmondsworth, UK: Penguin, 1971.

Background

Bancourt, Paul. *Les Musulmans dans les chansons de geste du cycle du roi*. 2 vols. Aix-en-Provence: Université de Provence, 1982.

Bloch, Marc. "Personal Liberty and Servitude in the Middle Ages, Particularly in

France: Contribution to a Class Study." In his *Slavery and Serfdom in the Middle Ages*, trans. William R. Beer, 33–91. Berkeley: University of California Press, 1975.

Friedman, John Block. *The Monstrous Races in Medieval Art and Thought*. 1982; repr. Syracuse: Syracuse University Press, 2000.

Geoffroy de Villehardouin. *La Conquête de Constantinople*. Edited by Natalis de Wally. 3rd ed. Paris: Firmin-Didot, 1882.

———. *The Conquest of Constantinople*. In *Chronicles of the Crusades*, trans. M. R. B. Shaw, 29–160. Harmondsworth, UK: Penguin, 1963.

Griffin, Robert. "*Aucassin et Nicolette* and the Albigensian Crusade." *Modern Language Quarterly* 26 (1965): 243–56.

Hahn, Thomas. "The Difference the Middle Ages Makes: Color and Race before the Modern World." *Journal of Medieval and Early Modern Studies* 31, no. 1 (2001): 1–37.

Heers, Jacques. *Esclaves et domestiques au Moyen Âge dans le monde méditerranéen*. Paris: Fayard, 1981.

Pegg, Mark Gregory. *The Corruption of Angels: The Great Inquisition of 1245–1246*. Princeton, NJ: Princeton University Press, 2001.

———. *A Most Holy War: The Albigensian Crusade and the Battle for Christendom*. Oxford: Oxford University Press, 2008.

Phillips, William D. *Slavery from Roman Times to the Early Transatlantic Trade*. Minneapolis: University of Minnesota Press, 1985.

Robert de Clari. *La Conquête de Constantinople*. Edited by Philippe Lauer. Paris: Champion, 1924.

———. *The Conquest of Constantinople*. Translated by Edgar Holmes McNeal. 1936; repr. New York: Norton, 1969.

Manuscript and Text

Blakley, Brian. "*Aucassin et Nicolette*, XXIV, 4." *French Studies* 22 (1968): 97–98.

Frank, Grace. "*Aucassin et Nicolette*, Line 2." *Romanic Review* 40 (1949): 161–64.

Simpson, James R. "Aucassin, Gauvain, and (Re)Ordering Paris, BnF, fr. 2168." *French Studies* 66, no. 4 (October 2012): 451–66.

Spitzer, Leo. "*Aucassin et Nicolette*, Line 2, Again." *Modern Philology* 48, no. 3 (February 1951): 154–56.

———. "Le Vers 2 d'*Aucassin et Nicolette* et le sens de la chantefable." *Modern Philology* 45, no. 1 (August 1947): 8–14.

Williams, J. Killa. "A Disputed Reading in *Aucassin et Nicolette*, I, 2." *Modern Language Review* 27 (1932): 62–63.

Date and Authorship

Ménard, Philippe. "La Composition d'*Aucassin et Nicolette.*" In *Mélanges de philologie et de littératures romanes offerts à Jeanne Wathelet-Willem*, ed. Jacques de Caluwé, 413–32. Liège: Cahiers de l'A.R.U. Lg., 1978.

Pelan, Margaret. "Le Deport du viel antif." *Neuphilologische Mitteilungen* 60 (1959): 180–85.

Genre and Form

Baader, Renate. "Ein Beispiel mundlicher Dichtung: *Aucassin et Nicolette.*" *Fabula* 15 (1974): 1–26.

Butterfield, Ardis. "*Aucassin et Nicolette* and Mixed Forms in Medieval French." In *Prosimetrum: Crosscultural Perspectives on Narrative in Prose and Verse*, ed. Joseph Harris and Karl Reichl, 67–98. Rochester, NY: Brewer, 1997.

Ch'en, Li-li. "Pien-wen, Chantefable and *Aucassin et Nicolette.*" *Comparative Literature* 23, no. 3 (Summer 1971): 255–61.

Pensom, Roger. "Form and Meaning in *Aucassin et Nicolette.*" In *Littera et Sensus: Essays on Form and Meaning in Medieval French Literature Presented to John Fox*, ed. D. A. Trotter, Robert Niklaus, and Keith Cameron, 63–72. Exeter: University of Exeter Press, 1989.

Porter, Laurence M. "The Problematics of Embedded Poems from Aucassin to Artaud." *French Literature Series* 18 (1991): 26–41.

Rea, John A. "The Form of *Aucassin et Nicolette.*" *Romance Notes* 15 (1974): 504–8.

Reinhard, John R. "The Literary Background of the *Chantefable.*" *Speculum* 1, no. 2 (April 1926): 157–69.

Rohr, Ruprecht. "Zu den Laissen in *Aucassin et Nicolette.*" *Romanistisches Jahrbuch* 11 (1960): 60–80.

Trotin, Jean. "Vers et prose dans *Aucassin et Nicolette.*" *Romania* 97 (1976): 481–508.

Woods, William S. "The Aube in *Aucassin et Nicolette.*" In *Mediaeval Studies in Honor of Urban Tigner Holmes, Jr.*, ed. John Mahoney and John Esten Keller, 209–15. Chapel Hill: University of North Carolina Press, 1965.

Performance

Frank, Grace. "The Cues in *Aucassin et Nicolette.*" *Modern Language Notes* 47, no. 1 (January 1932): 14–16.

———. *Medieval French Drama.* Oxford: Clarendon, 1954.

Furness, Clifton J. "The Interpretation and Probable Derivation of the Musical Notation in the *Aucassin et Nicolette* MS. (Paris, Bibl. Nat., fr. 2168)." *Modern Language Review* 24 (1929): 143–52.

Vitz, Evelyn Birge. "Variegated Performance of *Aucassin et Nicolette.*" In *Cultural*

Performances in Medieval France: Essays in Honor of Nancy Freeman Regalado, ed.
Eglal Doss-Quinby, Roberta L. Krueger, and E. Jane Burns, 235–45. Cambridge:
D. S. Brewer, 2007.

Winkler, E. "Or dient et content et fabloient." Zeitschrift für französische Sprache und
Literatur 64 (1941): 284–302. Repr. in Der altfranzösische höfische Roman, ed. Erich
Köhler, 267–88. Darmstadt: Wissenschaftliche Buchgesellschaft, 1978.

Linguistic Studies

Fonagy, I., and J. Fonagy. "Sur l'ordre des mots dans Aucassin et Nicolette." Bulletin de
la Société de Linguistique de Paris 64 (1969): 101–3.

Guiraud, Pierre. "L'Opposition actuel-virtuel: Remarques sur l'adverbe de
négation dans Aucassin et Nicolette." In Mélanges de linguistique romane et de
philologie médiévale offerts à M. Maurice Delbouille, 1:295–306. Gembloux: J.
Duculot, 1964.

Juneau, Marcel. "L'énigmatique 'waumone' dans Aucassin et Nicolette." Zeitschrift für
romanische Philologie 89 (1973): 447–49.

Kamimska, Alexandra. "La Valeur des pronoms personnels 'en' et 'y' dans Aucassin
et Nicolette, cantefable du moyen âge." Revue de Linguistique romane 29 (1965):
98–104.

Levy, Raphael. "L'Emploi du mot desport dans Aucassin et Nicolette." Modern
Language Notes 64, no. 3 (March 1949): 164–66.

Monsonégo, S. "Contribution statistique à l'étude de l'emploi des mots dans
Aucassin et Nicolette." Bulletin des Jeunes Romanistes 8 (1963): 37–42.

———. Étude stylo-statistique du vocabulaire des vers et de la prose dans la chantefable
"Aucassin et Nicolette." Paris: Klincksieck, 1966.

Moreau, François. "Note sur l'origine arabe du nom Aucassin." Nouvelle Revue
d'Onomastique 27–28 (1996): 53–54.

Roussel, Claude. "Mots d'emprunt et jeux de dupes dans Aucassin et Nicolette."
Romania 117, nos. 3–4 (1999): 423–47.

Schøsler, L. Le Temps du passé dans Aucassin et Nicolette: L'emploi du passé simple, du
passé composé, de l'imparfait et du présent 'historique' de l'indicatif. Odense, Denmark:
University of Odense, 1974.

Stewart, Joan Hinde. "Some Aspects of Verb Use in Aucassin et Nicolette." French
Review 50, no. 3 (February 1977): 429–36.

Szabics, Imre. "Moyens syntaxiques de l'expressivité poétique dans la chantefable
Aucassin et Nicolette." Acta Litteraria Academiae Scientiarum Hungaricae 17 (1975):
427–41.

Thomas, Michael Patrick. "The Diminutive World of Aucassin et Nicolette." Language
and Literature 16 (1991): 55–64.

Walter, Philippe. "Nicolas and Nicolette." Medieval Folklore 1 (Spring 1991): 57–93.

Sources, Analogues, and Literary Relations

Blondheim, D. S. "Additional Parallels to *Aucassin et Nicolette* VI, 26." *Modern Language Notes* 31, no. 8 (December 1916): 472–74.

———. "A Parallel to *Aucassin et Nicolette* VI, 26." *Modern Language Notes* 24, no. 3 (March 1909): 73–74.

Faral, Edmond. *Recherches sur les sources latines des contes et romans courtois du moyen âge*. Paris: Champion, 1913.

Goetinck, G. W. "*Aucassin et Nicolette* and Celtic Literature." *Zeitschrift für Celtische Philologie* 31 (1970): 224–29.

Hunt, Tony. "Precursors and Progenitors of *Aucassin et Nicolette*." *Studies in Philology* 74 (1977): 1–19.

Jodogne, Omer. "Aucassin et Nicolette: Clarisse et Florent." In *Mélanges de langue et de littérature du Moyen Age et de la Renaissance offerts à Jean Frappier par ses collègues, ses élèves et ses amis*, ed. Omer Jodogne, 1:453–81. Geneva: Droz, 1970.

Owen, D. D. R. "Chrétien, *Fergus*, *Aucassin et Nicolette*, and the Comedy of Reversal." In *Chrétien de Troyes and the Troubadours: Essays in Memory of the late Leslie Topsfield*, ed. P. S. Noble and Linda M. Paterson, 186–94. Cambridge: St. Catharine's College, 1984.

Scheludko, Dmitri. "Orientalisches in der altfranzösischen erzählenden Dichtung." *Zeitschrift für französische Sprache und Literatur* 51 (1928): 255–93.

———. "Zur Entstehungsgeschichte von *Aucassin et Nicolette*." *Zeitschrift für romanische Philologie* 42 (1922): 255–93.

Audience and Reception

Couvreur, Manuel. "D'*Aucassin et Nicolette* au *Chevalier du Soleil*: Grétry, Philidor et le roman en romances." In *Medievalism and manière gothique in Enlightenment France*, ed. Peter Damian-Grint, 124–51. Oxford: Voltaire Foundation, 2006.

Davis, Alex. "J. M. Synge's *Vita Vecchia* and *Aucassin et Nicolette*." *Notes and Queries* 58, no. 1 (March 2011): 125–26.

DuBruck, Edelgard. "The Audience of *Aucassin et Nicolete*: Confidant, Accomplice and Judge of Its Author." *Michigan Academician* 5, no. 2 (1972): 193–201.

Owen, D. D. R. "*Aucassin et Nicolette* and the Genesis of *Candide*." *Studies on Voltaire and the Eighteenth Century* 41 (1966): 203–17.

Schroeder, Klaus-Henning. "Zur Rezeptionsgeschichte von *Aucassin et Nicolette* seit dem 18. Jahrhundert." *Germanisch-Romanische Monatsschrift* 41, no. 2 (1991): 224–30.

Zygel-Basso, Aurélie. "Relire la chantefable au pays des fées: *Aucassin et Nicolette* (de la traduction de la Curne de Sainte-Palaye à *Étoilette* de Mademoiselle de Lubert, 1753–1753)." In *Influences et modèles étrangers en France sous l'Ancien Régime*, ed. Virginie Dufresne and Geneviève Langlois, 49–60. Québec: PU Lanval, 2009.

CRITICAL STUDIES

Angeli, Giovanna. "Le ambiguità dell' 'idillio' nei primi racconti francesi da *Piramus et Tisbé* à *Aucassin et Nicolette*." *Rivista di Letterature Moderne e Comparate* 59, no. 2 (April–June 2006): 137–50.

Bar, Francis. "Sur un épisode d'*Aucassin et Nicolette*." *Romania* 67 (1942–43): 369–70.

Bellenger, Yvonne. "*Aucassin et Nicolette*, ou le charme discret de l'insoumission." *Stanford French Review* 2 (1978): 47–50.

Bernabé Gil, Ma Luisa. "El viaje en la literatura medieval francesa: Ironía y fantasía en *Aucassin et Nicolette*." In *Medioevo y literatura*, I–IV, ed. Juan Paredes, 1:321–31. Granada: Universidad de Granada, 1995.

Brownlee, Kevin. "Discourse as Proueces in *Aucassin et Nicolette*." *Yale French Studies* 70 (1986): 167–82.

Clark, S. L., and Julian Wasserman. "Wisdom Buildeth a Hut: *Aucassin et Nicolette* as Christian Comedy." *Allegorica* 1, no. 1 (1976): 250–68.

Clevenger, Darnell H. "Torelore in *Aucassin et Nicolette*." *Romance Notes* 11 (1970): 656–65.

Conner, Wayne. "The Loge in *Aucassin et Nicolette*." *Romanic Review* 46 (1955): 81–89.

De Weever, Jacqueline. "Nicolette's Blackness—Lost in Translation." *Romance Notes* 34 (1994): 317–25.

Dorfman, Eugene. "Aucassin and the Pilgrim of 'Limousin': A Bilingual Pun." In *Linguistic and Literary Studies in Honor of Archibald A. Hill, IV: Linguistics and Literature; Sociolinguistics and Applied Linguistics*, ed. Mohammad Ali Jazayery, Edgar C. Polomé, and Werner Winter, 27–43. The Hague: Mouton, 1979.

———. "The Flower in the Bower: Garris in *Aucassin et Nicolette*." In *Studies in Honor of Mario A. Pei*, ed. John Fisher and Paul A. Gaeng, 77–87. Chapel Hill: University of North Carolina Press, 1972.

———. "The Lamp of Commandment in *Aucassin et Nicolette*." *Hebrew University Studies in Literature* 2 (1974): 30–72.

———. "The Sacred and the Profane in *Aucassin et Nicolette*." In *Homenaje a Robert A. Hall, Jr.: Ensayos linguisticos y filologicos para su sexagesimo aniversario*, ed. David Feldman, 117–31. Madrid: Playor, 1977.

Garreau, Joseph E. "Et si *Aucassin et Nicolette* n'était qu'une histoire d'amour fort simple." *Modern Language Studies* 15, no. 4 (Fall 1985): 184–93.

Gertz, SunHee Kim, and Paul S. Ropp. "Literary Women, Fiction, and Marginalization: Nicolette and Shuangqing." *Comparative Literature Studies* 35, no. 3 (1998): 219–54.

Gilbert, Jane. "The Practice of Gender in *Aucassin et Nicolette*." *Forum for Modern Language Studies* 33, no. 3 (July 1997): 217–28.

Green, Virginia M. "*Aucassin et Nicolette*: The Economics of Desire." *Neophilologus* 79, no. 2 (April 1995): 197–206.

Harden, Robert. "*Aucassin et Nicolette* as Parody." *Studies in Philology* 63 (1966): 1–9.

Houdeville-Augier, Michelle. "L'Autre et la violence dans *Aucassin et Nicolette*." In *La Violence dans le monde médiéval*, 282–92. Aix-en-Provence: Centre Universitaire d'Études et de Recherches Médiévales d'Aix, 1994.

Hunt, Tony. "La Parodie médiévale: Le cas d'*Aucassin et Nicolette*." *Romania* 100 (1979): 341–81.

Jewers, Caroline A. *Chivalric Fiction and the History of the Novel*. Gainesville: University Press of Florida, 2000.

Jodogne, Omer. "La Parodie et le pastiche dans '*Aucassin et Nicolette*.'" *Cahiers de l'Association Internationale des Études Françaises* 12 (1960): 53–65.

Kay, Sarah. "Genre, Parody, and Spectacle in *Aucassin et Nicolette* and Other Short Comic Tales." In *The Cambridge Companion to Medieval French Literature*, ed. Simon Gaunt and Sarah Kay, 167–80. Cambridge: Cambridge University Press, 2008.

Lacy, Norris J. "Courtliness and Comedy in *Aucassin et Nicolette*." In *Essays in Early French Literature Presented to Barbara M. Craig*, ed. Norris J. Lacy and Jerry C. Nash, 65–72. York, SC: French Literature Publications Company, 1982.

Liborio, Mariantonia. "*Aucassin et Nicolette*: I limiti di una parodia." *Cultura neolatina* 30 (1970): 156–71.

Lot-Borodine, Myrrha. *Le Roman idyllique au moyen âge*. 1913; repr. Geneva: Slatkine, 1972.

Martin, J. H. *Love's Fools: Aucassin, Troilus, Calisto, and the Parody of the Courtly Lover*. London: Tamesis, 1972.

McKean, M. Faith. "Torelore and Courtoisie." *Romance Notes* 3 (1961–62): 64–68.

Méla, Charles. "'C'est d'Aucassin et de Nicolette': L'objet du texte." In his *Blanchefleur et le saint homme ou la semblance des reliques: Étude comparé de littérature médiévale*, 47–73. Paris: Seuil, 1979.

Ménard, Philippe. *Le Rire et le sourire dans le roman courtois en France au moyen âge (1150–1250)*. Geneva: Droz, 1969.

Menocal, María Rosa. "Signs of the Times: Self, Other, and History in *Aucassin et Nicolette*." *Romanic Review* 80, no. 4 (November 1989): 497–511.

Micha, Alexandre. "En relisant *Aucassin et Nicolette*." *Moyen Age* 65 (1959): 279–92.

Musonda, Moses. "Le Thème du 'monde à l'envers' dans *Aucassin et Nicolette*." *Medioevo romanzo* 7 (1981): 22–36.

Pauphilet, Albert. *Le Legs du moyen âge: Études de littérature médiévale*. Melun: Librairie d'Argences, 1950.

Plangg, Guntram A. "Frage-Antwort Strukturen in *Aucassin et Nicolette*." In *Romanisches Mittelalter*, ed. Dieter Messner, Wolfgang Pöckl, and Angela Birner, 297–31. Göppingen, Germany: Kümmerle, 1981.

Rogger, Karl. "Étude descriptive de la chantefable *Aucassin et Nicolette*." *Zeitschrift für romanische Philologie* 67 (1951): 409–57; 70 (1954): 1–58.

Rossman, Vladimir R. *Perspectives of Irony in Medieval French Literature.* The Hague: Mouton, 1975.

Sansone, Giuseppe. *Idillio e ironia in "Aucassin et Nicolette."* Bari, Italy: Adriatica, 1950.

Sargent, Barbara Nelson. "Parody in *Aucassin et Nicolette*: Some Further Considerations." *French Review* 43, no. 4 (March 1970): 597–605.

Schneiderman, Leo. "Folkloristic Motifs in *Aucassin and Nicolette*." *Connecticut Review* 8, no. 1 (1975): 56–71.

Schreiner, Elisabeth. "Die aktive Rolle der Frau: Eine Untersuchung zu *Aucassin et Nicolette*." In *Berichte im Auftrag der Internationalen Arbeitsgemeinschaft für Forschung zum romanischen Volksbuch*, 85–101. Seekirchen: n.p., 1976.

Schroeder, Kalus-Henning. "Literatur des Übergangs: *Aucassin et Nicolette*." In *Festschrift für Rupprecht Rohr zum 60. Geburtstag*, ed. Wolfgang Bergerfurth, Erwin Diekmann, and Otto Winkelmann, 481–94. Heidelberg: Gross, 1979.

Schulze, Alfred. "Zum *Aucassin*." *Zeitscrift für französische Sprache und Literatur* 61 (1938): 205–10.

Secor, John R. "Le Porpenser: Forethought before Speech or Action in Tisbé and Nicolette." *Medieval Perspectives* 6 (1991): 76–86.

Smith, Barbara. "Toward an Interpretation of *Aucassin et Nicolette*." *Rendezvous* 3, no. 1 (1968): 43–59.

Smith, Nathaniel B. "*Aucassin et Nicolette* as Stylistic Comedy." *Kentucky Romance Quarterly* 26 (1979): 479–90.

———. "The Uncourtliness of Nicolette." In *Voices of Conscience: Essays on Medieval and Modern French Literature in Memory of James D. Powell and Rosemary Hodgins*, ed. Raymond J. Cormier and Eric Sellin, 169–82. Philadelphia: Temple University Press, 1977.

Spraycar, Rudy S. "Genre and Convention in *Aucassin et Nicolette*." *Romanic Review* 76, no. 1 (January 1985): 94–115.

Szabics, Imre. "Amour et prouesse dans *Aucassin et Nicolette*." In *Et c'est la fin pour quoi sommes ensemble: Hommage à Jean Dufournet*, ed. Jean-Claude Aubailly et al., 1341–49. Paris: Champion, 1993.

Taha-Abdelghany, Louisa. "*Aucassin et Nicolette* comme parodie de la chanson de geste." *Romance Review* 4, no. 1 (Spring 1994): 95–102.

Tattersall, Jill. "Shifting Perspectives and the Illusion of Reality in *Aucassin et Nicolette*." *French Studies* 38, no. 3 (July 1984): 257–67.

———. "Social Observation and Comment in *Aucassin et Nicolette*." *Neuphilologische Mitteilungen* 86, no. 4 (1985): 551–65.

Urwin, Kenneth. "The Setting of *Aucassin et Nicolette*." *Modern Language Review* 31 (1936): 403–5.

Vance, Eugene. "*Aucassin et Nicolette* and the Poetics of Discourse." In his *Mervelous Signals: Poetics and Sign Theory in the Middle Ages*, 152–83. Lincoln: University of Nebraska Press, 1986.

———. "*Aucassin et Nicolette* as a Medieval Comedy of Signification and Exchange."
   In *The Nature of Medieval Narrative*, ed. Minnette Grunmann-Gaudet and
   Robin F. Jones, 57–76. Lexington, KY: French Forum, 1980.
Williamson, Joan B. "Naming as a Source of Irony in 'Aucassin et Nicolette.'" *Studi
   Francesi*, n.s., 17 (1973): 401–9.